BOOK TWENTY-FIVE

WILL CAROLYN'S SUMMER JOB COST HER HER LIFE?

Carolyn's job as assistant to her friend's father, Nicholas Freeze, in his antique barn seems pleasant enough at first.

Then the discovery of a very old flask of murky liquid that carries with it the promise of eternal youth and a warning about its use awakens Nicholas Freeze's most miserly instincts. He sees the chance to make his fortune, and sacrifices everything – including his daughter's life – for it.

Carolyn, upset by her friend's death and the certainty that she is to be the next subject in Freeze's bizarre experiment, fails to notice that another, more frightening, menace has come to Collinwood... a strange, wolflike creature that also has her marked as a victim...

Hermes Press

Published by Hermes Press, an imprint of
Herman and Geer Communications, Inc.

Daniel Herman, Publisher
Troy Musguire, Production Manager
Eileen Sabrina Herman, Managing Editor
Alissa Fisher, Graphic Design
Kandice Hartner, Senior Editor

2100 Wilmington Road
Neshannock, Pennsylvania 16105
(724) 652-0511
www.HermesPress.com; info@hermespress.com

Book design by Eileen Sabrina Herman
First printing, 2022

LCCN applied for: 10 9 8 7 6 5 4 3 2 1 0
ISBN 978-1-61345-245-5
OCR and text editing by H + G Media and Eileen Sabrina Herman
Proof reading by Eileen Sabrina Herman and Feytaline McKinley

From Dan, Sabrina, and Jacob in memory of Al DeVivo

Acknowledgments: This book would not be possible without the help and encouragement of Jim Pierson and Curtis Holdings

Printed in Canada

Barnabas, Quentin and the Magic Potion
by Marilyn Ross

CONTENTS

CHAPTER 1 6

CHAPTER 2 18

CHAPTER 3 29

CHAPTER 4 40

CHAPTER 5 52

CHAPTER 6 64

CHAPTER 7 75

CHAPTER 8 86

CHAPTER 9 97

CHAPTER 10 108

CHAPTER 11 119

CHAPTER 12 130

CHAPTER 1

From the beginning Elizabeth Stoddard had been hesitant to allow her daughter, Carolyn, to take the summer job at the antique shop of Nicholas Freeze. Everyone in Collinsport regarded the elderly, dour proprietor of the barn antique gallery as odd and difficult to deal with. And when his young wife had left him some years back, after the birth of their only child, a little girl, no one blamed her. Nearly twenty years had passed since then and his wife was now dead. But his daughter, Hazel, who had attended a private school in Portland with Carolyn and been brought up by her mother's sister, was returning to the Maine coastal village of Collinsport for the summer. She planned to work as a clerk for her father and wrote asking Carolyn to join her.

Carolyn, in return, invited Hazel to be a guest at Collinwood, the great estate overlooking Collinsport Bay, during her stay in the village. When Hazel accepted, Carolyn at once began pressing her mother for permission to work in the ancient antique shop.

At first, Elizabeth had refused completely. "You'll have a dreadful summer working for that strange old man," she warned her daughter. "Nicholas Freeze has always been eccentric, and these last few years he has been more withdrawn than ever."

"But Hazel will be there working as well," Carolyn had

protested. "She's a wonderful girl, so her father can't be all that bad!"

"Hazel resembles her mother," Elizabeth replied.

"The pay he's offered me is good and I'd have fun working with Hazel," Carolyn pointed out.

"Nicholas Freeze is not likely to pay you well for work not done," was her mother's grim comment. "My opinion is that the work will be harder than you expect. And he has that drunken Tom Buzzell as his helper! I don't relish the idea of your being associated with such people."

"It will be an adventure," she insisted, without truly realizing what strange experiences the summer would bring her.

"Summer always means extra visitors here," Elizabeth reminded.

"But you have plenty of help without me."

"Barnabas is coming for the summer."

Carolyn smiled, knowing her mother had said this to help persuade her to remain at the estate instead of taking the job in the village. Barnabas was a favorite with her. Her mother's handsome cousin from England had taken an interest in her since her childhood, and despite the odd rumors which circulated about him, she had always found him pleasant.

She'd told her mother, "Barnabas will cause you no extra work. He will have his servant, Hare, with him, and they'll be living in the old house as usual."

Elizabeth had smiled. "It seems you are determined to spend your holidays in that musty old barn."

"I should be able to do as I wish," Carolyn pouted. "Uncle Roger is sending David to summer camp. It would be fun being with Hazel at her father's place every day and having her here in the evenings."

"The summer theatre will be in operation," her mother reminded her. "The new director, Mr. Buchanan, who is renting our cottage, told me he'd be glad to give you a position in the office or as a backstage worker."

It was a tempting offer, but Carolyn still hesitated. Mr. Buchanan, a quiet young man with a crew cut and dark glasses, had already settled in the cottage, and was beginning to prepare for the eight-week season at the theatre in the village town hall. She'd met him walking along the cliffs and her first impression was that he was strangely aloof. She couldn't imagine that it would be any easier to work for him than for Nicholas Freeze.

"I'd still prefer taking the job at the antique barn," Carolyn insisted.

Elizabeth sighed. "You can be stubborn when you like,

can't you? I'd say working in the theatre would be much more fun. Especially since Mr. Buchanan knows that Barnabas has worked on the stage in London, and has asked me to speak to him about appearing in some of the plays. Barnabas may well be one of the actors."

Carolyn said, "Then I'll go see Barnabas on the stage. I'll have nearly all my evenings free."

Elizabeth looked resigned. "Very well. I'll speak to Nicholas Freeze if you're not going to consider any other job offers. But I predict both you and his daughter will soon sicken of the work."

In a way this proved to be true, though Carolyn did find a certain fascination in the world of antiques. She went to work in the shop a week before Hazel arrived, in time to prepare for the July Fourth rush of tourists. The huge gray barn, with its open center door and plain white sign announcing, in uneven black lettering, "Olde Antique Barn" was a familiar sight to visitors driving into the village, and the white rooster weathervane on its peaked roof made the shop a landmark.

The weather-beaten white house in which Nicholas Freeze and his alcoholic assistant, Tom Buzzell, lived was situated in front of the barn and closer to the road. There was a wide roadway to the barn, gravelled but unpaved, and plenty of parking space on the grass in front of the gray building.

The barn was crowded with antiques of all kinds, ranging from ten-cent items such as pieces of broken colored glass of another era to fine mahogany chests and tables worth thousands of dollars. The small office and reception room was situated to the right of the barn door entrance, an untidy, dust-ridden place with a large old-fashioned safe in one corner. This was said to be the only true antique personally owned by Nicholas Freeze, who preferred to sell his vintage pieces and had a fine disdain for collectors as a group.

The second floor gallery was reached by open wooden steps, and was filled with everything from four-poster rope beds to Shaker rockers and brass inkwells. Part of the gallery was partitioned off into a room which was kept locked since it contained rare items and pieces on which Tom Buzzell was making repairs.

The first morning Carolyn reported for work, she met Tom Buzzell inside the doorway of the barn, where he was industriously restoring the finish of a Hepplewhite mahogany bowfront bureau. He paused in his labors to grin at her and ask, "You Elizabeth's girl?"

"I am," she said with a smile for him. "Is Mr. Freeze in?"

"You'll find him in the office," Tom Buzzell informed her

with a wink. "He likes to count his money first thing in the day. Makes him feel good."

She laughed. "I wonder what he wants me to do here?"

Tom, an emaciated, hollow-eyed man in shabby work clothes, gave the top of the bureau a furtive dab with his polishing rag. "Near as I can find out, he wants you and his daughter to greet customers and show them around. When it comes to any important sales, he'll take over. But you better go in and talk to him yourself."

"I suppose I should," she agreed. "Nice meeting you, Mr. Buzzell."

He chuckled. "Oh, you'll be seeing plenty of me except on weekends. I sort of take them off. But come Monday I'm always Johnny-on-the-job, whether I have a hangover or not."

Carolyn could think of no proper reply to this. She'd heard enough about his drinking bouts and his interest in spiritualism. One of the favorite stories of the town gossips was that as soon as Tom Buzzell got properly liquored-up at the Blue Whale Tavern he always buttonholed strangers and began telling them tales about the ghosts of the village.

When he was drinking, Tom was a firm believer in the supernatural. But when he sobered up, he seemed to forget all about this. Any Saturday night he could be found at the tavern, drinking with the newcomers to the village, giving them gruesome details of the haunted houses he'd known. Collinwood always played a prominent part in his stories. His favorite ghost was the Phantom Mariner, and he spoke darkly of the other weird inhabitants the old house had known: Barnabas Collins, who had been banished from the estate as a vampire, and who had gone to Britain to found the English branch of the family; the handsome Quentin, who could transform himself into a werewolf with ease, and who, some said, continued to return to the village in various disguises to conceal his identity. Though Quentin fought against this evil curse continually, he had never been able to conquer it and had remained unhappy and a wanderer.

Tom Buzzell had been blamed by Elizabeth for spreading rumors that the present Barnabas Collins also was a vampire. Barnabas's habit of appearing only after sunset and vanishing with the dawn had made the villagers suspicious of him. But Carolyn adored her distant cousin and was prepared to go on admiring him even if he were a victim of the vampire curse.

Now Carolyn left Tom and went to the glass-paneled door of the somber little office. As she waited for her knock to be answered, she peered through the dusty glass and saw the thin, white-haired Nicholas Freeze on his knees before the old safe, apparently locking it after returning his money. He turned and squinted at her with a stern look on his narrow, sallow face. Carolyn took one look at his great hook nose and decided that Hazel had surely not inherited her attractiveness from her father.

When Mr. Freeze opened the door, Carolyn introduced herself, "I'm Carolyn Collins."

His eyes, behind rimless spectacles, studied her closely. "You're a mite young for this business," he concluded.

"Your daughter, Hazel, and I are exactly the same age," she ventured. "And we're both interested in antiques."

"Know anything about them?" he demanded.

"I'm anxious to learn."

"You'd better, and fast," he said in his sour way. "You'll find a lot of books and catalogues over on the shelf there. Start now by studying them. You can take any of them home to read at night if you like."

"Thanks," she said.

"Most important part of this business is common sense," he went on tartly. "Our customers don't have a lot of it, so we need to have some extra."

Carolyn didn't know whether to smile or not, the stern old man with the reedy voice seemed so definite in his opinion. She couldn't be sure if he were making a joke or speaking his mind plainly.

She said, "I'll certainly try hard to get a knowledge of the business, and I know Hazel will, too. She's to arrive the first of the week, isn't she?"

He made his way over to the untidy shelf of books and blew the dust off them. Then, his back to her, he began rummaging through the big volumes.

"Yep. Hazel will get here early Monday," he said. "You're a good friend, she tells me. And it's mighty nice of you to have her stay at Collinwood as your guest."

"We had a grand time at school together."

Mr. Freeze turned to her and grimly said, "I haven't had anything to do with her bringing up. After her mother left me, it was her wish she be raised by her side of the family."

"She's a lovely girl. You must be proud of her."

Nicholas Freeze grunted. "I guess they done better than I would have, though it was me provided the money for everything. Hazel is my daughter, whether they like it or not That's one of the reasons I want her here this summer – to get to know her better."

"And she's anxious to work here," Carolyn said.

"Well, I hope it works out," he replied sourly. "You've met Tom Buzzell. He's my only other employee. He'd be one of the best in the antique business if he wasn't the town drunk."

"He's very agreeable," she said.

Mr. Freeze merely grunted again. "Begin with this book. It gives you a run-down of American and English antiques and average prices. When you're familiar with it, I'll take you around the barn and give you a test in recognizing some of the items you've read about"

She smiled timidly. "I'll try very hard."

"Sit down, then," he snapped. "There at my desk. I hardly ever use it myself."

Carolyn saw that it was rarely used indeed. The surface was cluttered with statements and bills of all sorts, most of them well covered with dust and grime. The desk calendar showed February of three years before, and the phone was almost buried beneath announcements and broadsides of auctions that had been hastily taken from their envelopes and tossed there.

Carolyn sat down in the black painted captain's chair behind the desk, and began to study the book, but Nicholas Freeze soon interrupted, "I hear your cousin Barnabas is coming here for the summer."

"Yes."

"I think it would be better for the village if he stayed away for good," he said scornfully.

Carolyn looked up from the book with surprise. "What makes you say that?"

"I don't much like the way he carries on," was his reply. "Roaming around the graveyards and the village streets at night like a ghost! Never showing himself in the daytime!"

"If he enjoys living that way, I don't see that he does anyone harm," she told him.

His rheumy blue eyes revealed malice. "I wouldn't be sure he does no harm. Tom Buzzell can tell you a story or two that might make your flesh go all goosepimples."

"I've heard some of the stories they tell about Barnabas," she said. "And I'm sure most of them aren't true."

"The first Barnabas Collins was a vampire," Nicholas Freeze reminded her. "That's why they got rid of him here."

"The present Barnabas is a nice person," she said, defending him. "Have you ever talked to him?"

Nicholas Freeze smiled nastily. "Oh, he's come by here every so often wearing his caped coat and carrying that cane of his like some country squire. I'm not one to be impressed by his fine airs."

"Then you do know him."

"Yes," he said, "and I knew the other one, that Quentin. Now there's a scoundrel if there ever was one. Not the sort of person you'd want to meet on the night of a full moon."

Carolyn was blushing. She said truthfully, "We never talk about Quentin at Collinwood."

"And no wonder," Mr. Freeze sneered. "He's come back here more than once pretending to be someone else. Each time, the countryside has been haunted by a werewolf."

Anxious not to get involved in any argument with her new boss, Carolyn did not reply. Instead, she gave her full attention to the book, and shortly afterwards she heard him go out and shut the door after him. She was beginning to wonder if perhaps her mother hadn't been right. Nicholas Freeze was going to be a difficult person to get along with.

Soon she forgot her annoyance in her study of the antiques book. She read of everything from furniture to antique glass and crystal. There were chapters on silver and porcelain and enamel. The morning passed quickly, and she'd only covered less than a third of the thick volume.

It was close to noon when the office door opened. She looked up and saw that it was the theatrical director, Mike Buchanan, who had entered. He was wearing light sport slacks and a yellow shirt open at the neck. His skin was tanned, and he had on dark glasses and a straw hat to protect him from the sun.

Coming to the desk, he said, "Mr. Freeze is out somewhere, and his helper told me I could talk with you."

She rose with a smile. "I'll help if I can. I'm new here."

"I don't want to buy anything," Mike Buchanan explained, "but I would like to borrow certain pieces every week for our stage settings. I'd be glad to see your firm get free advertising space in the program in return. And of course we'd send our truck to transport the things both ways, and we would be responsible for them."

Carolyn hesitated. She thought it would be a good arrangement for the shop, but knew she couldn't speak for Mr. Freeze. Still, she felt the serious young man should be encouraged.

"It sounds like a fine idea," she said. "I'll talk to Mr. Freeze about it if you like. I have an idea he may agree."

"I wish you would discuss it with him," Mike Buchanan said earnestly. "And if I don't hear from him, I'll drop by again."

"Please do," she said.

He studied her closely. "Aren't you from Collinwood?"

"Yes. I'm Carolyn Stoddard. Elizabeth is my mother. I've seen you on the grounds. You're renting our small cottage."

"I am," he said.

"I've often seen you walking along the cliffs."

"The view is magnificent," he said. "I envy you, living there all the time."

"It can be unpleasant and dull in winter," she said.

"The summer season makes up for it."

She smiled. "We like to think that. This is your first season directing the summer theatre here."

"Yes, and I hear you have a cousin from England who has acted professionally. I'm going to try and recruit him for the company."

"I hope you can persuade him," she said. "He's a handsome man. And I don't doubt he can act."

"I intend to discuss it with him as soon as he arrives. I understand that he will be living at the old house."

"Yes."

"I've heard he dislikes being bothered in the daytime?"

"He's writing a history of our family, and he is giving his days to that."

"Indeed?" Mike Buchanan raised an eyebrow and she thought his voice took on a mocking quality as he said, "I hope he hasn't forgotten to include the more colorful members of your family."

"Were any of my ancestors that colorful?"

He nodded. "I'd say so, from what I've heard. Surely you've heard the stories about Quentin Collins being a werewolf and Barnabas Collins a vampire."

"I don't believe it and I won't discuss it," she said.

"Oh?"

"I'm sorry."

"Perfectly all right," he said nonchalantly. "I didn't realize you felt so strongly about the matter. This is my first year here, and I have a lot of things to learn."

"I'll tell Mr. Freeze about your offer," she promised.

"Do that," he said, and started for the door. Part way there, he turned and said, "Come and watch rehearsals when we get under way. You'll be welcome anytime."

"Thank you. I'd like that."

The slim, tanned man nodded. "Well, good luck!" he said as he went on out.

Carolyn sat down with her book again, but found it hard to concentrate. The young man was very attractive and she'd liked him even though she hadn't wanted to talk family matters with him.

When Nicholas Freeze returned, she told him about the play director's visit and his offer. She ended by saying, "I said I thought you might be interested."

"I'll think about it," he said with such finality that Carolyn thought it best not to force the issue.

Her first several days at the cavernous antique shop were fairly uneventful. She found the subject fascinating and felt she was getting somewhere with her reading. She also took the trouble to tidy up the office and wash the windows. This made it much more pleasant. Nicholas Freeze barely grunted when he saw what she had done. Gratitude was apparently not one of his strong points. She couldn't see any resemblance between her friend Hazel's disposition and that of this old grouchy man who was her father.

There was a straggle of customers every day, though the main season hadn't begun. Carolyn had her first moment of glory when she sold a Heissey glass water pitcher and six glasses.

The old man had few friends. His two closest cronies were William Drape, the town undertaker, a thin scarecrow of a man who always dressed in rusty black, and Dr. Eric Blake, a semi-retired doctor addicted to drink. Every afternoon the three friends played cards in the office. At these times Carolyn was relegated to other tasks in the main area of the barn.

On one of these occasions, Tom Buzzell, busy fitting a new leg to a small marble-topped stand, paused in his work as she came by to say to her, "The boss having one of his card games again?"

She halted. She'd been on her way to dust some of the valuable vases. "Yes. Those other two men seem to come by at the same time every day."

"They count on the game," Tom Buzzell chuckled. "Will Drape has plenty of helpers at the undertaking parlor to do all his work, and Doc Blake has lost most of his practice because of his boozing, so he ain't busy."

"I guess Mr. Freeze needs their company," she suggested. "He must be a lonely man."

"He's lonely because he's cussed to get along with," Tom told her. "You're liable to find that out before the summer is over."

She smiled. "His daughter will soon be here. He'll probably behave his best for her."

"Now I wouldn't want you to count on that, Miss Collins," Tom Buzzell said. "If he'd been nicer to her mother, she wouldn't have left him. There was too much age difference between them two, and Nicholas wasn't of a mind to change his ways."

"It's too bad," she said.

"Yep," Tom said. "I've got an idea the spirits of them he's hurt and cheated haunt him. That's what makes him so ugly all the time. Don't you think he sort of looks like he's being taunted by ghosts?"

"I couldn't say," she replied tactfully.

But on the following wet afternoon, when Mr. Freeze took her through the shadowed old barn, stopping at various points to have her identify an antique and give her approximate idea of its value, she recalled his helper's words. It was true that the thin, sallow face of Nicholas Freeze bore a haunted look.

Pausing before a black walnut chest, he asked, "What's the period?"

She hesitated. "Victorian?"

"Right," he said glumly as he moved further into the shadows. The barn was especially eerie now; it was dark and raining, and the pattering of rain on the roof sounded loud. He stopped by a secretary desk. "Well?"

She studied it nervously. "Queen Anne," she suggested.

"It is," he said as if disappointed. Then he indicated a jug. "What about that?"

"A Bennington," she said.

"You've done your homework well," he admitted reluctantly. "Hope Hazel catches on as quickly."

"I'm sure she will," Carolyn said. "She's very bright." He grunted again and led her on to other tests. Occasionally she made a mistake, but mostly she was able to identify the various items. When it was over, she felt like a full-fledged apprentice, though her employer gave her no word of praise.

Carolyn was anticipating the arrival of the old man's daughter on Monday. She had enjoyed the pleasant, blonde girl at school and was delighted she was going to stay at Collinwood. Elizabeth was a little worried that Nicholas Freeze resented his daughter's not staying with him.

She told Carolyn, "When I talked with that sullen old man he made some nasty comments about Hazel coming here."

"But he has no place for her," Carolyn protested. "He lives in that old, run-down house by the barn. And every weekend Tom Buzzell gets drunk there. Hazel couldn't put up with that."

"I suppose not," Elizabeth sighed. "Still, I think he isn't happy about it."

On Friday evening Nicholas Freeze asked Carolyn if she would stay late. She was only supposed to work days, but told him she would stay on for the evening if she was provided with transportation back to Collinwood.

"I'll have Tom Buzzell drive you home in the truck," he promised, and Carolyn agreed to remain.

During the evening a load of furniture arrived from an old house in Ellsworth. Nicholas Freeze was very excited about it, but Tom Buzzell looked angry and nervous and didn't seem very interested. He helped him unload the items and carry them up carefully to the locked room on the second floor.

When the work was over, Nicholas Freeze came into the office rubbing his hands with delight. "A real find!" he told her. "Belongings of a family dating back to the early seventeen-hundreds. First man of science to ever settle in this area. I've bought up his journals and possessions for a song from a stupid young woman who is the last of the line and wanted to sell the stuff to buy furniture for herself and her husband. I'm going over the items tonight personally. A fine trade."

She said, "It's getting late. Will Tom drive me home now?"

Nicholas Freeze frowned at this interruption of his thoughts. "Oh, yes, I suppose so. Go out and ask him."

Leaving the office, she went in search of his helper. But he was nowhere in sight. And when she checked the house, he wasn't there, either. Somewhat despairingly she returned to the office and told Mr. Freeze, "I can't find Tom. I think he may have left for the tavern."

Her employer looked grim. "Come to think of it, he was behaving thirsty," he said. "I guess we can't expect him back, and as I don't drive the truck myself you'll have to find other transportation."

"It may not be easy," she said.

"Should be someone going out your way," Freeze said in a tone that indicated he had no further interest in what he considered strictly her problem despite his promises.

She saw there was nothing to be gained in arguing with him. She left the shop and hurried to the main street. Then she suddenly remembered that the play director, Mike Buchanan, who was rehearsing in the city hall auditorium, had invited her to come by for rehearsals any time. She could watch the rehearsal and then drive back to Collinwood with him in the sports car she'd seen him driving.

Heartened by this idea, she walked more swiftly until she reached the old brick building which had the town offices on its lower floor and a small auditorium on the second level. It seemed dark and deserted, but there was a light on in the hallway. She mounted the stairs and found herself standing at the rear of the one-hundred-and-fifty-seat theatre. It seemed she was too late – the rehearsal had ended and the theatre was empty. The rehearsal had probably just ended, or the place would be locked up.

Carolyn stood in the silent auditorium, which was dark except for a single light on a stand on the stage. Its glow cut the gloom on the stage and the first few rows of seats but left the balance of the auditorium in blackness. She was about to leave when she suddenly was flooded with a sensation of fear, fear of some unknown thing. She stood there in alarm, wanting to leave but frozen by her fright.

Then she thought she heard someone moving about halfway down the auditorium on the left. Her terrified eyes fixed swiftly on that spot. For a moment, nothing seemed to disturb the shadows. And then suddenly a figure rose up from between the rows of seats – a figure so frightening that she at once reacted with a scream. It was a man with the distorted features of an animal! A man with a wolf-like face! And he was coming toward her!

CHAPTER 2

She gazed in frozen horror at the hideous-faced creature advancing to her through the murky shadows of the silent auditorium. Then with another scream she turned and made for the steep stairway leading down to the exit. And as she did, she almost collided with someone on the way up. It was Barnabas Collins!

"Carolyn!" There was surprise in his voice as he prevented her from falling.

"Barnabas!" she cried with a sob of relief.

"What is it?" Barnabas held her in his arms.

She turned and glanced up to the top of the stairway with a frightened look on her lovely face. "Back there! A weird, ugly thing rose up between the seats and came after me. It looked like a man with a wolf's face!"

Barnabas looked incredulous. "Are you sure you're not imagining this?"

"No! I saw something!"

"I'll take a look," he suggested.

"Be careful!"

His smile was tolerant. "I'm sure I'll find nothing up there to harm me," he said.

"You think I was hysterical for no reason."

"No, but things often take on a different appearance in a lonely, dark place. I'll have a look for myself." Barnabas let her go and started up the stairs.

"I'm going along," Carolyn said, making a sudden decision.

"Perhaps you'd better not," he warned her.

"No. I'm going, too," she insisted.

They entered the auditorium together. It was still mostly in darkness except for the single night lamp on the stage. Barnabas marched down the center aisle toward the stage, and Carolyn followed him rather timorously. There was no sign of the macabre figure which had terrified her, though she half expected to see it appear again from some dark corner.

Barnabas was down by the stage now, his sallow, handsome face highlighted by the night light. His erect bearing made him a figure of assurance, and all her fears were eased through merely being with him. He searched the stage with his deep-set, keen eyes. "Anyone there?" he called out.

There was no reply from the shadows.

Carolyn moved closer to him. "It's no use," she said. "Let's leave here at once."

Barnabas gave her a meaningful glance. "Be patient a moment," he said and called out again, "Who is back there?"

Carolyn expected no more results from his enquiry than there had been previously. But she was due for a surprise. After a delay of a few seconds, there was a rustle of movement from the left of the stage and then a figure emerged from the shadows.

Carolyn involuntarily gasped as a young man walked out to the middle of the stage.

But this was no terrifying ogre with the features of a wolf, but a rather thick-set, long-haired young man with a broad, yet pleasant, face. He gazed down at them in a puzzled fashion.

"Yes?" he asked.

Barnabas said, "How long have you been here? We're looking for someone who gave this young lady a bad scare."

The young man seemed puzzled. "I don't know what you're talking about. There's no one in the theatre but me, and I was downstairs in my dressing room. I only came up here when I heard you shouting."

Barnabas didn't seem convinced. "You're certain there's no one else here?"

"I am," he said. "Our director, Mike Buchanan, was the last to leave. We were chatting in my dressing room about the opening tomorrow night. He left and I stayed down there for a while to do some last-minute studying of lines."

Barnabas asked, "So no one could have been in the auditorium?"

The actor shrugged. "Unless they came up by way of the main stairway as you did. I wouldn't know about that, since I was downstairs in my dressing room, as I've told you."

"I see," Barnabas said.

The young man was staring at them curiously. "May I ask what your business is here?"

Carolyn felt it was time she spoke up, "Mr. Buchanan invited me here to watch rehearsals any time I liked. I hoped that I might find one going on. But when I arrived, the auditorium seemed empty. Then a strange figure came at me from the shadows and terrified me."

The young man listened with polite sympathy. "I'm sorry you had such a bad experience."

Barnabas said, "My name is Barnabas Collins and I came by to speak to Mr. Buchanan about playing some parts with your company."

He smiled. "Of course. You're the actor from London."

"And this is my cousin, Carolyn Stoddard," Barnabas introduced her.

"I'm Jim Swift," the young man said, in a much more friendly tone. "I'm playing most of the leads this season. And I'm happy to meet you both." He turned to Carolyn. "Sorry you had an unpleasant experience here. Maybe somebody came in from the street. There are still a few hobos around this area in the summer."

"Whoever it was didn't look human," she said with a tiny shiver.

"I suppose that the shadows could have distorted the face of whomever she saw. That and the presence of some intruder may explain what happened," Barnabas said.

Carolyn frowned. "If that is so, how did he get away?"

"A good point," Barnabas said. "Are there any side exits?"

Jim Swift pointed to the right of the darkened auditorium. "There's one over there. It leads down a fire escape."

Barnabas quickly went up the aisle and through a row of seats to the door. He tested it and then called back to them, "It's not latched. I'd say someone has used it lately." He glanced outside and then came in and closed the door again. Returning to Carolyn, he said, "Whoever it was is a long way from here now."

"They've surely used that door for their getaway. Sorry it happened." Jim Swift smiled at her. "Don't let it keep you away. Things aren't usually that scary here."

"I'll try to believe that," she said with a wan smile.

"Is this your first theatre experience in Maine?" Barnabas asked the actor.

He nodded. "Yes. I've worked mostly in New York. I answered an advertisement Mike Buchanan put out asking for actors. I wanted to get away from the city for the summer."

"You won't find any place much more pleasant than here," Barnabas said.

"Tell Mr. Buchanan I'll be by to see him after the performance tomorrow evening."

"You may see him at Collinwood. He's living in the summer cottage," Carolyn told him.

"Perhaps I will," Barnabas agreed. And to the young man, he said, "We'll be talking to you another time."

"I hope so," Jim Swift smiled. "I've enjoyed meeting both of you."

They left the actor still standing on the stage and went downstairs and out into the darkness of the street. Barnabas stood there a moment, as if taking stock, then said, "Does the hotel still serve food in the evenings?"

"Yes. Are you hungry?"

"No," he answered, "but I thought you might be."

"I'd rather have something cool to drink."

Barnabas smiled at her. "That sounds as if the Blue Whale Tavern was indicated."

They made their way down the steep slope of the main street to the neon lights of the Blue Whale Tavern. As usual, it was crowded with people of all ages, most of them tourists visiting the quaint fishing village. Barnabas attracted the stares of many in his Carnaby Street mod-type cape and with his silver wolfs-head black cane. He made an elegant, striking figure as he escorted her to a booth in the rear of the noisy, smoke-filled place.

As they sat down, he glanced at the blaring, neon-lighted jukebox and the several couples doing a frog-like dance in front of it.

"I can never accustom myself to that kind of music," he complained.

"It is noisy," she said.

"I like something with a bit more melody," Barnabas told her. The waitress came and he ordered beer and a soft drink. Then giving her one of his melancholy smiles, he said, "It's good to see you again, even if our meeting was a trifle unusual."

"I heard you were coming, and I was so pleased."

"Elizabeth tells me you're working for Nicholas Freeze this summer."

"Yes. I know his daughter, Hazel. She's very nice – not at all like him."

"I would hope not," Barnabas said dryly. "Nicholas is not one of my favorite people. Still, you'll probably find the antique business interesting."

"I do," she agreed. "But he's not very reliable. He promised I'd have a drive home if I worked tonight. Then his man, Tom Buzzell, went off to get drunk as he does every weekend, and I was left stranded. That's why I went to the auditorium. I hoped I might find Mike Buchanan there and get a ride back home."

"Sounds like a typical Nicholas Freeze trick," Barnabas said. "What about this Buchanan? Do you like him?"

"He seems friendly," she said. "But he is quiet and retiring." She sighed as the waitress brought them their cold drinks and some chips. "I still don't know what to make of that figure in the auditorium."

Barnabas gave her a questioning glance. "You say the face had the look of a wild animal?"

"It made me think of a wolf."

His black eyes fixed on hers in a hypnotic manner. "I wonder if perhaps Cousin Quentin isn't back?"

This astonished her. "I never thought of him!"

"Your description made it sound so much like Quentin," Barnabas said.

"Elizabeth and Roger hoped he would never return."

"But he has, so many times," Barnabas said. "He's a master of disguise and sly enough to know when he is least likely to be suspected. Coming here in summer when the place is filled with tourists would be ideal. He could mingle with the others and not be noticed."

His words alarmed her. "You think that Quentin might have been lurking up there?"

"Possibly. He might have seen you enter the building and then come up by way of the fire escape so that he was hiding there when you reached the auditorium level."

"It could have been him," she agreed. "He's probably on the street again now acting like an ordinary tourist."

"That's the way he works," Barnabas said. "Of course, there is another interesting possibility."

She stared at him. "What?"

"What was your impression of that actor, Jim Swift?"

She looked surprised. "He was very nice. Why?"

"He could be Quentin, you know."

"I'd never thought of that."

Barnabas said, "There's something about him that reminds me of Quentin. I'd like to check his past and find out his history."

"That's why you asked him all those questions?"

"Yes," Barnabas said. "But he didn't really tell me anything about himself, did he?"

"Not beyond the fact that he found the job through an advertisement," she remembered.

"So the logical thing will be to question Buchanan and see what he can tell us."

"That won't be difficult," she said.

"On the other hand, he may not know much about this Swift. He probably hired him in a hurry."

Carolyn considered it all. "I somehow don't think the monster I saw was Jim Swift. I think the body of the man was taller and slimmer."

"It would be hard to be sure in those shadows."

"I know," she worried. "I prefer the theory that whoever it was came from the street."

"And that could have happened," Barnabas said.

Carolyn hoped it had been that way. She liked Jim Swift too much to want him to turn out to be the renegade cousin of the Collins family. She said to Barnabas, "You think it was the werewolf figure I saw?"

"I'm afraid so."

"That has to mean more trouble at Collinwood."

"Not necessarily so," Barnabas said. "Often Quentin is restrained in his behavior here. He simply has the desire to return to his home area. But there are times when the curse takes control of him and he becomes a werewolf against his will. That could have been what happened tonight."

"Now I'm really worried about getting home," she said.

"You needn't be," Barnabas smiled. "I'll see that you have transportation."

When they finished their drinks, he escorted her to the street and up as far as the hotel again. There he hailed one of Ed Muller's two town taxis and helped her in it for the drive back to Collinwood.

"Aren't you going home now?" she asked.

"Not yet. I have a few things to do. I'll see you tomorrow night."

"Thank you," she said. "You shouldn't have bothered."

"I couldn't do less than see you reach home safely," Barnabas said. "And the next time Nicholas Freeze asks you to work in the evening, I'd refuse him."

"I will," she promised. "Things will be different after his daughter gets here on Monday. I'll have company." Barnabas said goodnight and closed the door of the taxi, and she was on her way to Collinwood. The driver was an elderly man whom she knew by sight, though she couldn't remember his name.

"Dark kind of night," he said, as he headed the taxi out of the village.

"Yes," she agreed. "Much too dark to walk the lonely roads home."

"You shouldn't ever do that," the driver warned her. "Too many bad things have happened here in the last few years. You're Elizabeth's daughter, aren't you?"

She leaned forward in the seat slightly. "Yes."

"Hasn't your Uncle Roger got a daughter, too?"

"No. He has a son, younger than me. His name is David. He's at summer camp this year."

"Good place for a boy," the man said as he swiftly drove along the narrow road. "And you're working for Nicholas Freeze?"

"Yes."

"He's a crazy old man," the driver said with disgust. "He's got plenty of money and yet he's stingy. You won't get much extra pay there. The only one he can get to work for him regular is Tom Buzzell. He's lucky to get a job anywhere, being a wicked drunk."

"It's too bad about Tom," she agreed.

The driver kept his eyes on the winding road as they neared Collinwood. "And that was Barnabas Collins hired the cab, wasn't it?"

"Yes."

"He hasn't been back here for a while."

"He usually comes during the summer," she said, wishing the man would stop asking questions about the family.

"Kind of peculiar, ain't he?" the driver suggested. "People say he wanders around the cemetery in the middle of the night."

Carolyn was annoyed. "He does take long walks at night. It may be he visits the cemetery along with other places. I don't see that there's anything wrong in that."

"Maybe not," he said, realizing he'd gone too far. "It's just most people wouldn't think of wandering around gravestones after dark. I guess it takes all kinds."

Carolyn did not answer. She knew the sly insinuations the driver was making. He'd heard the gossip in town that the present Barnabas Collins was tainted with the curse of his ancestor, and that he also was doomed to walk by night only, to seek out prey to satisfy his thirst for blood. She had listened to the stories whispered about her handsome cousin from England, but she'd refused to take them seriously. She didn't care what Barnabas was – she was very fond of him.

The taxi came to a halt in front of Collinwood and the driver let her out. "Hope you make out all right at the antique shop," were his parting words.

She went into the house and found her mother, Elizabeth, waiting for her in the living room. Glancing up from the novel she was reading, Elizabeth said, "I've been worried about you. What kept you so late?"

"Nicholas Freeze asked me to work some extra time," she explained and went into all the details of what had happened.

"I've been afraid of that Nicholas Freeze," Elizabeth worried. "I know he can't be relied on. I'm sorry you've taken the job."

"It will be better after Monday when Hazel is here."

"I hope so. I must remember to thank Barnabas for seeing that you were sent safely home."

Carolyn gave her mother an ironic smile. "It seems to me it wasn't too long ago that both you and Uncle Roger were warning me to be careful of Barnabas. I think you allow yourselves to become much too concerned."

"There was a time when Barnabas caused us concern," her mother replied. "Some things that have happened here are beyond your understanding."

Carolyn didn't pursue the subject further. She was content to go upstairs to bed. She fell asleep at once, but she had a series of bad dreams. In them she returned to the dark, silent theatre and was again confronted by the monster with the grotesque animal features. She twisted restlessly between the cool sheets, moaning as she was tormented by her nightmare. And in the morning she awoke to still have vivid memories of those frightening moments.

At breakfast her mother announced, "Your Uncle Roger has decided you're to have the use of the old station wagon while you're working this summer."

"That will be wonderful," she said. "Then I won't have to worry about getting back and forth."

Elizabeth eyed her sternly. "I'll expect you to be careful in your driving. One accident and I'll insist the car is taken from you and you quit that job. I want you to remember that."

"I will," she said. "I'll be really cautious."

She meant to be. Having a car of her own for the summer would make it much more pleasant for her. She left Collinwood shortly before nine, since she was due at the antique shop by nine or a little after.

She hadn't driven far on the side road when she came upon the theatrical director, Mike Buchanan, in tweed suit and with bare head, walking briskly in the direction of the village.

She braked the station wagon to a stop beside him and leaning across the seat asked him, "Can I give you a lift into the village?"

The good-looking man with the heavy sunglasses smiled. "Thanks," he said. "I'm just taking a walk for my health. I'll use my own car when I drive into rehearsal. None of my people are up this early."

"You apparently don't mind early rising," she said.

"I don't," he agreed. "I like this morning stroll."

"I went to the theatre late last night, but I just missed you," she told him.

"Sorry," he said. "And I was there late talking with Jim Swift."

"So he told me. He's new to the company, isn't he?"

The director nodded. "Yes. I hired him in New York recently."

"He seems very nice," she said. "Do you know him well?"

Mike Buchanan shook his head. "No. I know less about him than I do many others in the company. But he is an excellent actor, and I'm sure he'll be popular with the theatregoers here."

"I'd say so," she agreed. "I had a strange experience in the theatre last night. Some tramp appeared from a dark corner and really frightened me. He had a horrible face."

Buchanan frowned. "Does Jim Swift know about this?"

"Yes. I told him."

"Good," he said, "he'll probably give me an account of it when I see him later. We'll take steps to see that strangers don't get in the theatre. Be sure and come back some time when we're rehearsing."

"My cousin Barnabas was there to see you last night," she said. "He asked me to tell you he'll come to the theatre again tonight. I think he'd like to join the company."

"And we're anxious to have him. Could I talk to him this morning?"

"You'd better wait," she warned. "He rarely goes out or sees anyone during the day."

Mike Buchanan looked puzzled. "I see," he said. "Then I'll let the matter rest until he visits the theatre."

"That would be best," Carolyn said with a smile. "I spoke to my employer about providing the antiques for your stage settings, and while he didn't give me any real answer, I have an idea it will be all right."

"Thank you," Mike said. "I'll make it a point to see him before next week's play."

With that she drove on into the village. She parked her car behind the barn and then went inside to the office. Nicholas Freeze was at his desk reading what seemed to be some ancient manuscript. When she came in, he looked up rather guiltily and closed the manuscript at once.

"Tom Buzzell hasn't shown up," he told her. "I doubt if we'll see him until Monday morning – it will take him until then to sober up. Trade should be brisk today, since the summer people are mostly all here."

"What do you want me to do first?" she asked.

"You can dust some of the furniture and keep an eye open for customers. If you want me, I'll be here," the old man said in his reedy voice.

"Very well," she said and left him to find a dust cloth and begin on some of the larger pieces of furniture close to the entrance of the barn, which seemed to gather the most dust. As she worked she wondered what Nicholas Freeze had been reading in the office. He'd acted strangely secretive when she walked in.

There were only two customers in the next half-hour, and

neither of them made any large purchase. One bought an ancient plate with a nursery rhyme on it and the other a set of cut-glass salt and pepper shakers. She knew the prices on these and attended to the sales herself without bothering Nicholas Freeze.

Gradually she worked her way up the steep steps to the balcony. Here the sun's rays rarely reached the clutter of furniture and other items. She moved along a narrow passage amid the gloomy shadows, occasionally dusting a vase or lamp, but it was a thankless task. So much grime had collected here over the years only a little could be removed from the surface. She came to the door of the room where Nicholas Freeze kept his most valuable items and noticed that it wasn't locked. The padlock was hanging open on the door. Apparently when he'd last been inspecting the new shipment of antique furniture he'd neglected to lock the door on leaving.

She remembered his telling her that this was an especially valuable lot of goods that included the possessions of a chemist of nearly three centuries ago. Filled with curiosity, she opened the door a little. It creaked in protest but gave way, and she found herself in a partitioned-off area with only a small dust-ridden window high up on the barn wall to give it any light. Most of the room was in dark shadow.

Just now the sun streamed down through the gloom in a limited ray to focus directly on a Chippendale cherry inlaid slant-top desk with an ogee bracket base. She was fascinated by the rare old item and went over to inspect it. She dusted it lightly and examined it more closely. It was while she was dusting the interior of it that her hand must have touched a hidden spring, for a secret panel at once opened, revealing three dusty glass bottles with wide bases and narrow necks. They were ancient in design, and their glass stoppers had been sealed in place with wax.

She judged each of the glass containers must hold about a half-pint of some dark liquid. She took them out of the secret compartment one at a time and carefully removed the dust from them. She had no idea what the bottles might contain or why they had been so carefully hidden, but she was certain they had been there for a very long while. The modern-day owners of the ancient piece probably never knew they were there.

Carolyn debated whether to put them back where she'd found them and close the compartment without saying anything or report her discovery to Nicholas Freeze. She hardly knew what the old eccentric's reaction would be. He could become angry with her for entering this private area, or he might be grateful for her discovery of the hidden compartment and its contents.

After hesitating a moment, she decided to return the bottles and close the secret compartment. No doubt Nicholas Freeze would make the discovery later by himself when he was going over the various pieces more carefully. She was placing the first of the bottles back again when her hand touched something. It was an envelope of obvious age.

Carolyn removed the envelope, which was yellowed and stained by the years. There was no writing on it, and it was unsealed. When she opened it, she saw it contained a single folded sheet of writing paper. Very carefully she removed the paper and unfolded it.

The writing was crabbed and small, and time had faded it to a pale brown. The spelling was also very different from that of the present day and made the short message doubly difficult to understand. But the signature stood out bold and clear, "John Wykcliffe, Esquire." The date after it was January 11th, 1724.

Carolyn was becoming more and more excited about her discovery. She frowned in concentration as she attempted to get some meaning from the letter. It seemed to be a message warning someone about the contents of the bottles. The gist of it was that the fluid contained in them was an elixir capable of prolonging life indefinitely. That it must be administered in extremely minute doses, and even then there was an element of danger in the rare liquid.

She read and reread the stiff, almost foreign, sentences with their other-century spellings. Her hand trembled slightly as she picked up one of the odd-looking bottles again to inspect it more closely. She was thrilled by the discovery that some ancient alchemist had distilled this murky, thick liquid with the belief that he had found the secret of eternal youth. No doubt he was long since dead, but he had left behind this wistful evidence of his belief that in his experiments he had somehow stumbled on the secret of extending life and youth.

She returned the letter to its envelope and was about to place the missive back in the secret compartment again when suddenly a skeleton-like hand pounced out of nowhere to seize her wrist and send a cold surge of horror through her!

CHAPTER 3

Carolyn turned to gaze into the angry face of Nicholas Freeze. The old antique dealer snapped, "How dare you come in here snooping!"

Recovering from her shock, she said, "I didn't mean any harm."

"Give me that letter," the irate old man demanded as he snatched it from her.

"I was dusting this desk when I accidentally happened on a secret compartment," she explained nervously. It was apparent that Freeze was going to be as difficult as possible.

"You had no right to come in here!"

"I didn't realize that," she said.

"I have my most valuable stock in here, and I protect it by keeping the area under lock and key."

"It was the fact you'd neglected to lock the door that attracted my attention."

Mr. Freeze looked uncomfortable. "In the future you are not to enter here, whether the door is open or not. Do you understand?"

"Yes."

"Very well, then," he said. "You can go downstairs to wait on any customers while I set things to rights up here. Don't call me unless I'm really needed."

"Yes, sir," Carolyn said quietly, delighted at being let off so easily. For a few minutes she'd worried that she would be fired.

He waved her out impatiently. "Then, get along!" She left hastily, glad to get away from him. As she went out he was reading the ancient letter. The three containers of the murky liquid stood on the desk in front of him. She felt he'd been unreasonable in his attitude but wasn't surprised by this. The letter about the elixir of youth had fascinated her, and she determined to discuss it with Barnabas. He had been working on a history of the family for some time and would know about the period of John Wykcliffe.

Some tourists came by in search of antique china and silver. She sold a gold Limoges dessert set and a silver teapot, sugar and creamer by Bailey Banks. Old Nicholas Freeze came down in time to discover her wrapping up the silver set for the second customer and seemed well pleased. When they were alone, he apologized for his anger upstairs and commended her for her swiftness in learning the basics of the business.

"You've done very well," he said, "and when Hazel arrives on Monday I'll count on you to help teach her some of the things you've learned."

That evening Carolyn drove home in the station wagon pleased with her job and at having the use of the car. She'd almost forgotten about the weird experience she'd had at the antique shop that morning until she met Barnabas in the garden at dusk.

"Did you have an interesting day?" he asked with a smile.

And then she remembered. "A strange one," she said, and told him of discovering the bottles and the letter and ended by asking him, "Did you ever hear of a John Wykcliffe?"

He considered. "A family by that name lived in Ellsworth."

"That's the one."

"They've about all died off," Barnabas said.

"I know," she agreed. "And Nicholas Freeze got that desk from the old house. He bought it along with a lot of other things."

"John Wykcliffe was surely a chemist of note," Barnabas told her. "He was responsible for several formulas still in use today, but I doubt very much if he found an elixir of life."

"Many people have tried to discover some magic compound for that purpose but no one has succeeded thus far," she said.

"There are a couple of specialists in Europe who make extravagant claims for their preparations," Barnabas said with a bitter smile. "But I have small faith in them."

As they stood in the dusk together she asked him, "What do you think old Nicholas Freeze will do with the bottles of the elixir?"

"It wouldn't surprise me if he tried to make some enormous profit on them," Barnabas said.

"You may be right. He was in a wonderfully good humor when

he came down from the gallery, but when I left him up there he'd been angry. Perhaps the idea of being able to commercialize on the elixir cheered him up."

"It could be, yet I don't see how he'd manage it."

"He's cunning and miserly. If there's a way, he'll probably find it."

"In the first place, the elixir is undoubtedly useless. And in the second, where would he merchandise it? He'd find few customers among his hard-headed friends in Collinsport."

She remembered, "There was something else in the letter – it mentioned that the liquid could be dangerous."

"Most such potions are," Barnabas agreed. "I think our good friend Nicholas would be wise to ignore the letter and empty those bottles down the drain."

"I wonder if he will," Carolyn mused.

"You got home safely last night?" Barnabas asked.

"Yes, but the taxi driver made me angry."

"Why?"

"By insinuating you might be a dangerous character. He did a lot of silly rambling about vampires."

His deep-set eyes met hers. "And about my being one?"

"It was very tiresome. And I let him know I thought so."

Barnabas smiled bleakly. "Thanks for defending me. I'm not sure that I deserve it."

Carolyn was indignant. "I remember the silly stories some of those village girls told about being attacked and bitten on the throat. They only wanted to attract attention to themselves. None of them died from the experience."

"The bite of a vampire need not cause fatal results," Barnabas told her.

Carolyn gave him a warning look. "Don't make any confessions to me, Barnabas. I don't want to hear them."

He smiled sadly. "You're willing to accept me for what I am?"

"Always," she said stoutly.

He touched a hand to her arm tenderly. "I have few friends as loyal as you, little cousin."

"I wish we weren't cousins," she said, suddenly forlorn. "If you were merely a handsome stranger, I could fall in love with you."

"And where would that lead?"

"We'd run away together and be married and live happily ever after," she said.

Barnabas laughed softly. "That's almost as much a fantasy as the elixir of life that you found in that old desk. I doubt if I ever shall have the privilege of settling down to married life."

"You will when you meet the right girl."

His eyes met hers sadly. "I have known many lovely girls. Any one of them might have made me a good wife. But fate has ordained me to be a wanderer. It wouldn't be fair of me to marry anyone."

"I'd marry you, cousin or not," Carolyn said emphatically. "Anyway we're such distant cousins I can't think that it matters."

Barnabas touched his lips to her forehead, and she was acutely conscious of the coldness of his kiss. He said, "You stand high on my list, little one. If there should be a change in my way of life I'll seriously consider your offer."

She was staring at him. "Why are your lips so cold?"

"I'd prefer not to talk about that," he said.

"Very well. I'll change the subject," Carolyn said. "What about the theatre company? Do you plan to take on any roles?"

"Perhaps some minor ones," Barnabas said, "though I will be unable to play any matinees. I would insist they have an understudy for any daytime performances."

"They usually have one, anyway, don't they?"

"Most of the time."

"I spoke to the director this morning. He was out for a stroll. Are you going to the theatre tonight?"

"I think not," Barnabas said with a slight frown. "I have some other matters to look after. But I may try to catch him at the cottage when he returns after the show. We can discuss things there as well as anyplace else."

"I suppose so," she agreed.

He loomed above her in the fading light, concern on his handsome face. "I'm not satisfied about what happened to you in the auditorium last night. There has to be some better explanation of it."

"I'd almost forgotten."

"Better not," he warned. "You could be in danger. Watch that Jim Swift if he tries to become friendly with you."

"You still think he might be Quentin?"

"Or some other twisted character leading a double life," was his opinion. "Did you learn anything more about him when you talked with Mike Buchanan today?"

"No. He hasn't much information about his past."

"Just as I expected," Barnabas said. "If I see Buchanan later, I'll question him some more."

"I wish you'd stay here with me for the evening," Carolyn said. "I'm lonely."

"I'd like to, but I can't," Barnabas told her. "I'm going to the village for a little while. If I have time, I might drop in and see Nicholas Freeze. Perhaps he'll tell me about the elixir."

"I doubt that," she said.

Barnabas left her, and she went inside to read. Her book was interesting, and she remained cosily perched on a sofa in the rear parlor with it for most of the evening. It was eleven-thirty before she realized how late it was and put aside the book. She guessed that her mother and Roger were likely in bed by this time. She was able to sit up late because tomorrow was Sunday and she didn't have to report for work.

On Monday Hazel Freeze would arrive for the summer, and she not only would have a helper at work, she would have company at Collinwood. Hazel would be staying with her until she left in September. It was a happy prospect, and once again she marveled that an elderly, caustic man such as Nicholas Freeze should have such a sweet daughter.

Her thoughts were interrupted by the rumblings of distant thunder. And as she sat there heavy rain began hitting the window. In a few moments there was a sharp flash of lightning, and then more thunder. An electrical storm of real dimension had developed, as often happened in Maine at this season of the year.

She had a morbid interest in such storms, and she especially liked to see the lightning flash over the ocean. So she got up and walked down the dark corridor to the front of the house. All the lights were out, and it was only then she realized the electricity had gone off during her brief moments in the corridor. This didn't disturb her, as the power often went off only to come on again in a few minutes, or at the worst after the storm had ended.

She went to the window in the entrance hall and pushed aside the curtain. She stared out into the rainy darkness and watched for the next flash of lightning. It came sooner than she expected, a dazzling blue forked flash streaking above the turbulent angry waves of the ocean.

The thunder was loud, and the rain continued. It was a wretched night, and she began wondering where Barnabas might be. She hoped he wasn't caught out in the storm somewhere. He'd spoken of coming back to talk to Mike Buchanan at the cottage and so would probably be there at about this time. She pictured the broad-shouldered, caped Barnabas striding along in the storm, the lightning outlining his gallant figure against the night

Then the lightning blazed across the pitch darkness of the sky once more. Carolyn had another brief glimpse of the sea with its white-capped tall waves. It was at that instant she had her first feeling that she was not alone. Terror shot through her like a pain at her first intimation of a supernatural presence in the house! And to make her plight more frightening, there were no lights to turn on.

She tried to remember where there might be candles. At least a lighted candle would give her a slight feeling of assurance. Her mind worked quickly and she had a vision of the two tall white candles on the sideboard in the living room, not too far from the doorway. Elizabeth always kept matches in the top drawer. It was all coming back to her.

The thunder growled ominously and then exploded in a loud cannon-like roar. Lightning came once again, and she still remained frozen by the window in the hall. She lacked the courage to walk the dozen or so steps through the darkness into the living room to find the candles.

Why was she suddenly so craven? What was it that had made this reasonless fear coil around her stealthily like some obscene serpent? It was nothing that she had heard or seen, but rather an almost instant sense of something not being right in the house. Of an unseen presence near her and watching her! All the tales of ghosts and phantoms plaguing Collinwood came back to her at this moment. Which of them was staring at her from the shadows, soundless and unseen? Which one among all those restless and unhappy spirits of past generations of the Collins clan had been summoned by the fury of the storm?

She was convinced that close at hand this spirit presence lurked, ready to reach out from the shadows with a clammy touch and place its wicked spell on her. The rain came once more in a torrent, and the thunder and lightning eased. She was trembling, but some small part of her courage returned and she made her way across the entrance hall with faltering steps. As she reached the doorway to the living room she again had a strong feeling of a phantom presence, but she would not turn back.

She moved into the almost pitch-black living room and groped for the sideboard. The thunder rumbled, and a great flash of lightning brought everything in the big room into clarity. She uttered a frightened cry, for standing there gazing at the portrait of a dark beauty was the figure of a man!

He turned at her cry, and she had a fleeting glimpse of his face before the blaze of lightning faded. It was the actor, Jim Swift! The same one who had been on the stage of the theatre the night before when she'd seen the monster with the wolf-like face.

His presence in the house startled her, but his being there served to explain her strange feelings. Now she reached the sideboard and quickly pulled out the top drawer and found the matches. A second later she was applying a lighted match to one of the candles set out there. Then, taking the candlestick in hand, she went over to confront the actor.

"Did I frighten you?" he asked, his pleasant features showing a smile in the glow of the candle.

"You did. I had no idea there was anyone in here."

"I was studying one of the portraits when the lights went out."

She stared at him hard as the candle flickered slightly, causing strange shadows on his face. "May I ask how you got in here?"

"The front door was open, and I let myself in. Oh, I tried the bell twice, but no one answered. It was raining very hard, and I didn't want to remain on the steps." Carolyn listened and felt he couldn't be telling the truth. If the bell had rung twice, surely she would have heard it.

Somewhat accusingly, she said, "I was in the parlor at the back of the house, and I didn't hear it."

He continued to study her with that mocking smile. "Perhaps the thunder blotted the sound out."

"Perhaps," she said, though she still didn't believe it. But she couldn't do anything but accept his story or flatly call him a liar. At this point she preferred not to do that.

"I drove to the cottage with Mike," the actor said. "He invited me to spend the night there with him."

"I see."

"Then that Englishman who was with you the other night came by. The storm hadn't broken yet."

"Barnabas."

"Yes. I knew they had some business to discuss, so I decided to take a stroll. I remembered that you lived here and it seemed a good idea to come up and chat for a few minutes. About that time the rain began, and I was drenched by the time I reached your door."

"That's too bad," she said, relenting a little in the face of his story. He made it seem very reasonable. Perhaps the thunder had prevented the bell from being heard.

His eyes held a twinkle with the candlelight reflecting in them. "I'm not the type to stand on the doorstep getting soaked when the door isn't locked. I came in and saw no one."

"I'm the only one who is still up."

"I saw the living room was lighted, so I came in here. The first thing that caught my eye was the portrait of that fascinating dark girl. She reminded me of photographs I've seen of my mother when she was young."

"You must mean Angelique," she said, holding up the candle to cast some of its soft glow on the portrait.

He was gazing at the painting now. "She's something wonderful!"

"She played a strange role in the story of the Collins family," Carolyn told him.

"Of course she lived a very long time ago."

"Centuries ago."

"The artist surely captured her beauty," the young actor said.

"There is a legend that she was in love with the ancestor of the

Barnabas Collins you've met, and that, in a jealous mood, she placed a curse on him."

Jim Swift glanced at her. "What sort of curse?"

"I don't know all the facts of the story," she said quickly, not wanting to get into a discussion about vampires.

"It sounds interesting. I'm sure she was a strong person."

"From what they tell, she must have been," Carolyn agreed.

There was a weak flash of lightning and the thunder rumbled farther away now. He said, "I think the worst of the storm is over."

"I hope so."

He stared at her. "Are you afraid of lightning?"

"Not really, but it's scary when the electricity goes off."

Jim smiled again. "This house was built for candlelight."

It was the way he said it that struck her as strange. She said, "You talk as if you were familiar with the house, as if you'd been here before," all the while thinking, can this be Quentin? Has he returned again, this time disguised as a young actor?

"Of course I never have," he said.

"Are you sure?"

His face held an expression of mocking irony. "Quite sure," he said in a quiet voice.

But his very words left a taunting doubt in her mind. She went on, "And is this your first visit to Collinsport?"

"It's my first visit to Maine."

"I hope you like it."

"I'm sure I shall," Jim Swift said. "At another time I'd like to have a more complete tour of this house."

"I'll be glad to show it to you," she said. "Perhaps you'll have a chance to come back in the morning."

"I doubt that. We have an early rehearsal."

"Well, there'll be other opportunities, since you'll be in the village the entire summer."

"I hope to."

She said, "It would be nice if Mr. Buchanan and Barnabas can come to terms. I've never seen him act."

"I'm positive Mike wants to hire him. It may all be arranged by now."

Carolyn stood there holding the candle and feeling rather awkward. She said, "I'd like to hear about your career, learn more about you."

"My story isn't interesting," he said cagily.

"It must be!" she insisted.

"I'm not the kind of person who likes talking about himself," he told her. "I know that's odd in an actor, but it happens to be true."

Again she became suspicious of him. He was clearly trying to avoid giving any details of his life. Why should he take this attitude if he didn't have something to conceal?

She said, "You claim this is your first visit to Maine."

He smiled. "I not only claim it, it happens to be the truth."

Her cheeks warmed. He knew what she was thinking. He had guessed her suspicions and was taunting her. She said, "Where were you born? And where have you lived most of your life?"

"My birthplace was a small town in Vermont," he said, "and most of my life has been spent in New York City, the only place an actor can find regular work. But even there it's not always available."

"You've not worked with any of the actors in this company before?" she said.

"No. They're all strangers to me."

He said it as if to let her know she'd not discover any information about him from that source. With a wise look, she said, "I think you like that. You enjoy keeping all the facts about yourself secret. Being an enigma to everyone."

"I believe it does make an actor more interesting."

"I thought that must be your theory," she said, though she privately believed there was more to it than that and that he was clinging to this veil of secrecy to keep them from finding out that he was Quentin Collins.

Looking at him very directly, she said, "The Collins family has spread far and wide. It's a wonder you haven't met some of us before. Especially Barnabas, since he's in the theatre. He had a feeling he'd met you somewhere." It could have been a shadow cast by the flickering light of the candle, but Carolyn was almost certain she'd seen him flinch slightly. Then in his usual poised fashion he gave her another smile.

"I'm positive I've never met him. I wouldn't be likely to forget such a striking personality."

She was ready for her main thrust, and her eyes meeting his, she asked, "Did you ever meet anyone called Quentin Collins?"

He was completely assured this time. "I don't believe so. Would he be an elderly man?"

"He's young," she said. "About your age."

Jim Swift showed wry amusement. "I'm not as young as you may think."

"I'd still say he'd be about your age."

"The name doesn't mean anything to me. Is he also in show business?"

"No, but he travels a great deal. I thought you might have met him somewhere."

"Not that I know of," he said mockingly. "You've been asking me so many questions about myself I haven't been able to find out anything about you."

"I've led a very simple life. There's no story."

"Everyone has a story," he said.

"Mine is just living here and school," she said. "I have a friend from my boarding-school days coming to spend the summer with me, Hazel Freeze."

His eyebrows lifted. "Is she related to the Nicholas Freeze who has the antique place?"

"Yes, she's his daughter."

"That's an interesting place," the young actor said. "I guess we're going to borrow some stage properties from the old man."

"I'm trying to arrange it," she said.

As she spoke, the lights came on dimly, and then the two great cut-glass chandeliers in the room returned to full strength. She at once blew out the candle and placed the holder on a nearby table.

Jim smiled and said, "I'd call the lights my cue. It's time for me to leave. Sorry I frightened you prowling around in here in the dark."

"You're forgiven," she said. "And do come back again."

"And don't you forget you've been invited to the theatre anytime. I hope the scare you received there won't stop you from coming back."

"I think not."

"Mike Buchanan was very upset about that. He's making sure no one has a chance to wander into the theatre like that again. Without a question, it was one of that gang of hippies who are living on the Collinsport beach. I hear the town authorities are pretty upset about them."

"I can understand that," she said.

He cast a final glance at the portrait of Angelique. "I'd like to hear the complete story about her some time."

"I'll try and collect all the facts for you," she said as they moved toward the entrance hall.

"Perhaps your cousin Barnabas can give them to me," he suggested. "He has his portrait out here."

"How did you know that?" she asked at once.

He gazed up at the portrait of Barnabas that hung high on the rear wall of the shadowed hall. "I saw it when I first came in."

She doubted that this could be true, with the hall in near darkness as it was. Again she had the feeling that the young man knew the house and had been in it many times before.

"It's a likeness of his ancestor, the first Barnabas Collins," she said. "Though our Barnabas does resemble him."

"I didn't realize that," Jim said. "You're right. The resemblance is startling."

"I'll see you again," she said as he opened the door a little.

"You surely will," he agreed, his eyes meeting hers. And then taking her completely by surprise he reached out and drew her to him for a kiss. In a twinkling he released her so that she hardly knew what had happened. As she stared at him in confusion, he told her, "Whenever I say goodnight to a pretty girl, I kiss her."

"I'm glad you've warned me," she said, blushing. "I'll not be so surprised next time."

He laughed "I think we're going to have a great summer, Carolyn." And with that he went out into the night.

She stood on the steps watching after him for a moment. When he was a little distance away, so that his figure was barely more than a vague shadow in the darkness, he turned and waved to her. She waved back, and he continued on toward the cottage.

Carolyn went inside and closed and locked the door. She was still in a confused state of mind concerning the young man's visit. It could be that he was simply the young actor Jim Swift, but she still worried that it might be Quentin returned in a new role.

She went up to bed, and the night passed uneventfully. But when she came downstairs for a late breakfast on Sunday morning, she found her mother and her Uncle Roger facing each other tensely in the entrance hall.

Knowing something was wrong at once, she asked, "What's happened?"

Her mother stood there pale and agitated. "Nothing for you to worry about," she said.

But Roger was in one of his ugly moods. "I'd say it's something for all of us to worry about! It seems Barnabas is out to get himself in trouble!"

CHAPTER 4

Knowing her Uncle Roger's tendency to temper fits, she felt a wave of fear for Barnabas. Once Roger got an idea in his head, it wasn't easy to reason with him, and apparently something had convinced him that Barnabas was guilty of a misdemeanor.

"What's wrong?" she asked.

Roger's face was beet-red. "There's just been a report on the radio of a girl found walking in a dazed state along the beach last night. She seems to have been one of the hippie crowd living on the beach. According to the report, she remembers being suddenly attacked by someone, after which her mind went blank. Aside from shock, there were apparently no other injuries." He paused and then spoke slowly so that his remaining words would be sure to sink in. "But there was an odd red mark on her throat"

Elizabeth spoke up, "That doesn't have to mean anything!"

Roger turned on her angrily. "Not if you want to play ostrich and stick your head in the sand and ignore the facts around you. It's clear enough to me. Barnabas is up to his old tricks. He attacked that girl for her blood!"

"The mark could have been caused in some other way," Carolyn ventured.

Her uncle smiled coldly. "Then who attacked her, and why?"

"I wouldn't know," she said, with a sigh.

"It isn't up to us to worry about it," Elizabeth said. "If the police decide that Barnabas may be to blame, they'll get after him soon enough."

"It won't be long until the rumors spread around the village," Roger declared. "There'll be dozens of people who remember the last escapades of Barnabas and why he left here so hurriedly. Once they know he's back again, they'll not be slow in placing the blame on him."

"Even though he mightn't be guilty," Carolyn said.

"I don't think there is any doubt that he is," Roger replied. "He'll have to be warned to stop this business or leave Collinsport at once. I won't have him living here and disgracing the family!"

"I think you should have more proof of his guilt before you accuse him," Carolyn said with a troubled look on her attractive face. She could see that Roger was ready to act on this impetuously.

"What has happened in the past is proof enough for me," Roger declared angrily.

Her mother's face was pale. "Wait and see if any other incidents occur," she begged her brother. "Carolyn may be right. This could be an isolated case which suggests the happenings before but which has nothing to do with them. Barnabas may never have set eyes on that unfortunate girl."

Roger glared at her. "I find that hard to believe."

"I don't think Barnabas was in the village last night," Carolyn said. "He was at the cottage talking to the director of the playhouse, Mike Buchanan, while the storm was on."

"How do you know that?" Roger demanded.

"One of the actors came to the house to visit me."

Her uncle frowned. "At that hour of the night?"

"I was up reading. It was all right."

Elizabeth now looked worried. "I didn't hear anyone come in."

She said, "No doubt the sounds of the storm drowned out the doorbell and our voices as we talked."

"Who was this fellow?" Roger asked.

"His name is Jim Swift. He said when he left the cottage Barnabas was there talking to the director about joining the company."

Roger still looked unconvinced. "It will depend on what time Barnabas was with this Buchanan and when that girl was attacked. He could have been involved with her before or after his interview with Buchanan."

"I'd say that is unlikely," Elizabeth said.

"I'm taking nothing back until I know for sure. As far as I'm concerned, Barnabas is guilty until he proves himself innocent," Roger said as he turned on his heel and strode off down the hallway toward his study.

After he'd left them, Elizabeth sighed deeply. "I'm afraid this means trouble for Barnabas."

Carolyn asked, "Why is Uncle Roger so ready to blame him?"

"They've never got on too well," her mother reminded her.

"It's so unfair!"

"I agree," Elizabeth said, "but that won't change anything. Barnabas should be warned."

"Perhaps he'll pay us a visit tonight," she said.

"I suppose that's the earliest we can hope to see him," her mother agreed. "I only wish I could discuss it with him right now."

"But he never leaves Collinwood during the day."

"I know," her mother sighed.

"I'm sure he was with that director most of the evening," Carolyn said, wanting to put the best light on things.

"I hope it turns out that way," Elizabeth said, but there was doubt in her voice.

As soon as Carolyn finished breakfast she decided to walk to the cottage that Mike Buchanan had rented and see if he was there. She meant to try and find out how long Barnabas had been at the cottage, and the time of his arrival and departure. She also looked forward to the possibility that the pleasant, if somewhat mysterious, young actor Jim Swift might be there. It would be fun talking to him again.

It was a pleasant, sunny morning, and she covered the short distance to the cottage in less than ten minutes. But when she got there it was locked, and there was no sign of the director's sports car, so she assumed that both he and Jim Swift must have gone on to the village. They were probably having a rehearsal later in the morning. Disappointed, she turned and walked back along the cliffs toward Collinwood.

As she made her way along the path that followed the uneven line of the cliffs, she gave the problem some thought, and by the time she'd reached the great sprawling, dark mansion of Collinwood she'd come to a conclusion. She would try and get into the old house and leave a message for Barnabas, even if she wasn't able to talk to him. In this way he would be prepared for the trouble awaiting him.

If the stories about his being a vampire were true, he would be sleeping during the daylight hours. But she could write her message and leave it for him. The catch was that Hare, the burly, mute servant who looked after Barnabas, would try to prevent her from getting near him. She would need a streak of luck to get by the stolid Hare.

But this didn't deter her from making an attempt. Leaving the cliff path, she took the one that went by the stables and other outbuildings and led to the old house occupied by Barnabas and his faithful servant. On this Sunday morning there was little activity on the grounds. She saw no one at the stables, and a strange calm was in the air.

As she neared the old house she suddenly halted, and her face lighted up with pleased excitement when she saw the stocky figure of Hare vanishing over the hill in the direction of the old family burial ground. She had no idea what his mission might be there. The important thing was that it had taken him away from the house for a while. Perhaps for long enough for her to find a means to enter it and reach Barnabas or leave him a message.

She moved on as soon as Hare vanished and began to consider her plans. It would be too much to expect to find either the front or back door unlocked. But there was a cellar entrance on the right side of the ancient building and she might be able to get in through it. There was usually a padlock on it, but the wood was old and rotten, and using something to force the fittings, she might be able to break them away. It was a desperate course to take, but she was that anxious to reach Barnabas.

When she reached the shuttered, red brick structure known as the old house, she mounted the several steps to the front door and used the rapper to announce her presence. She waited, but there was no reply. Either Barnabas hadn't heard it, or he was truly sleeping that sleep which, according to the vampire legend, so much resembled death.

With a sigh Carolyn went down the steps and stood for a moment staring across the field to make sure that Hare had continued on his way. She assumed this must be so, since he was no longer anywhere in sight. Satisfied that she wouldn't be disturbed for at least a little while, she went to the flat, weathered wooden doors that led to the cellar. A rusty padlock was on them, but this didn't worry her too much. She searched around behind the house until she found a length of thin, rusted pipe to pry the lock open with.

Going back to the flat, gray doors, she inserted the pipe under the fittings and then used all her strength to break them away from the rotten wood. She strained for a moment, and feeling the fittings give slightly, kept up the pressure until there was a splintering of the ancient wood and the fittings were free on one side. She could now lift the doors open with ease to reveal the dark, gaping entrance to the cellar at the bottom of some worn stone steps.

To keep Hare from noticing the doors had been forced, if he returned soon, she had to carefully lower them back in place after she'd gone down the steps. This left her in a sudden, frightening darkness. Blinded by the change from the bright sunshine, she groped her way into the damp staleness of the cellar. She moved carefully along the earthen floor attempting to get her bearings.

Then toward the rear of the cellar she saw an open door with a faint ray of light showing through. This served as a beacon to guide her along the length of the cellar's shadows. The silence and darkness had cast an eerie spell on her. She began to wonder if she had been too confident in embarking on her mission. Had she been too reckless? Did she really understand the meaning of the curse from which Barnabas suffered? Only her deep affection for the handsome Britisher allowed her to go through this effort to give him a warning.

The fetid darkness of the cellar was all around her, and she slowly made her way toward that open doorway with its pale light. She stumbled over a small box, and her taut nerves made her cry out. Quickly recovering herself and stepping out around it, she continued on.

Now the door was only a dozen feet away. There was a rustling sound and a frightened squeak, and her horrified eyes saw the blurred outline of a huge rat as it scurried across the floor in front of her. She halted at the sight of it and almost turned and ran back to the cellar doors and freedom, but she was too near her destination to retreat.

She pushed on to the doorway and then inside the shadowy room she saw the oaken coffin with its brass handles set out on a stand. That was all the furniture in the room. At the head and foot of the coffin, candles flickered in brass candlesticks. The upper portion of the casket was open, and as she moved closer, a step at a time, she finally saw the sallow face of Barnabas. He lay sleeping peacefully, his head on a satin pillow.

She gasped as she came to stand by the casket. He could be dead! There was no sign of breathing. His hands folded on his chest had the waxy look of death. The shadows created by the flickering of the candles added to the awesomeness of it all. With his eyes closed Barnabas lost much of the magic of his charm, though there still was a classic nobility to his features.

This left little doubt that the legends she'd heard were true. She'd been inclined to believe all along that Barnabas suffered the same vampire curse as his ancestor. But she hadn't been faced with this side of it until now. With trembling fingers she drew her small notebook from her pocket and prepared to write a message of warning on it and leave it in his hands so that he would find it immediately on waking, which, according to the legend, wouldn't be until dusk.

She hastily scrawled the note for him, realizing that Hare could return at any time and she would then be forced to cope with the angry servant. Finishing the message, she signed her name. Then she nervously slipped it between the wax like fingers of his clasped hands. At this moment she found it hard to believe that Barnabas would ever return to life. He was so much the corpse. And yet she realized he must spend each day in this fashion. When darkness came, he would once more be the vibrant, assured cousin she had come to admire.

Bracing herself with this thought, she lingered by the casket for a final moment, staring down at the sallow, familiar face. Then she heard a sound behind her, and her whole being was chilled with fear. She waited, unable to move for a moment. What she had heard had resembled a stealthy footstep. She had immediate visions of an enraged Hare behind her.

There was silence again, and she waited, staring with terrified eyes at the sleeping Barnabas in his coffin. No hope of aid there. He was helpless when he succumbed to this rest of the dead. She had to battle this through on her own. Perhaps she'd only imagined the sound; it could be a matter of nerves.

With a deep breath she tried to collect herself and then very gradually turned to stare in the direction from which the sound had come. And there, only a short distance in the room behind her, stood Mike Buchanan, still wearing his dark glasses in spite of the gloomy surroundings. She was amazed to see him there.

"How did you get down here?" she gasped.

His smile was cool. "I followed you."

"You had no right!"

The director nodded toward the casket. "Are you bothered because I've found out about him?"

"You shouldn't be here."

He came nearer to her and said easily, "I'd call that a matter of opinion. I doubt if you have any right here yourself."

"That's different," she said. "I came here with a message."

"A message for the dead?" His tone was mocking.

"Barnabas isn't dead," she said, a tremor in her voice.

Buchanan moved over to her. "No need to take a belligerent attitude. I'm your friend. And the condition of Barnabas is deeply interesting to me."

"You shouldn't have intruded! This is no business of yours!"

Mike Buchanan gave her another of those annoying smiles. "Don't panic! I mean him no harm! I'm on your side."

"Then go!"

"Not yet."

"Neither of us should be here," she protested nervously. "If his servant comes back, there is liable to be terrible trouble."

"You risked that when you came here."

"I intended to leave right away," she said.

"And so we will, once I get a good look at your vampire friend," he said. "I think I'll stage a performance of the play Dracula and cast him in the lead. Think what a lot of publicity we could get – actual vampire playing the part of stage vampire! We could draw audiences from all over!"

"It's nothing to joke about," she said with some anger.

Mike looked injured. "I wasn't making fun. I'm thinking of a perfect bit of casting."

"I'll have to tell Barnabas about you forcing your way in here," she warned him.

"If I were you, I wouldn't," he told her.

"Why?"

"It will only upset him without doing any good," he replied. "We met and talked last night. He's agreed to play in at least three of our plays. Doing that could be excellent for him, and help keep him in a normal frame of mind. If you scare him off by telling him I know his secret, he'll back out of the bargain. That would only hurt him."

She stared at him. "I won't allow you to exploit him as a freak!"

"I was only joking about that."

"How can I be sure?"

"You have my word," Mike said. "I told you I was on your side. But I guessed what you were up to when I saw you breaking into this cellar, especially after you became so indignant when I mentioned earlier about the vampire and werewolf legends."

Carolyn said, "We try not to talk about such things with strangers."

"Must you consider me a stranger?"

"You are one."

"No longer." The director smirked as he gazed at the immobile features of Barnabas in the casket. "I was ready to believe there was nothing to that vampire legend, but now I have actual proof."

"Not really," she said, wanting to get rid of him.

"And what about the other one? The werewolf?"

"I don't know what you're talking about," she bluffed.

He smiled, showing his even white teeth against his tanned face. "Don't try to act innocent. You know who I'm talking about. Quentin!"

"I have never met Quentin."

"Next you'll be telling me you wouldn't recognize him if you did meet him," he said with some derision.

"That's true."

"I have an idea the Collins family are leagued together to keep outsiders in doubt. You know what is going on, but you want to keep it a secret for the good of the family name," Mike accused.

Carolyn moved a step away from the casket. "I want to get out of here at once. Hare will be coming back."

"Before I go, I'd like to discover what made you risk coming down here. What was the message you had for our sleeping friend?" As he spoke, he reached into the casket and whisked the slip of paper with her written message from Barnabas's wax like fingers.

Carolyn attempted to grasp the paper from him, but he held it away. She said, "It's personal. You have no right to read it!"

"Take it easy," he said. "I want to help you. I'm your friend, and I can't assist unless you let me."

"I don't need your help."

"You may change your mind," Mike warned her. "It will do no harm for me to know all that's going on. Then I'll be in a better position to advise you."

"Read it if you like," she said despairingly. "It won't do you any good!"

He was already scanning the note. A slow smile spread across his face. "Just as I told you before. You Collinses are working together to protect yourselves from scandal. So Barnabas attacked a girl last night?"

"No. I can't say that. It's just that my Uncle Roger thinks he did. I wanted to warn Barnabas."

"The chances are he did attack her. In his state he needs a regular supply of human blood. You must know enough about vampires to realize that."

"Barnabas was with you last night!"

"Only for about an hour, from eleven-thirty to shortly after midnight. He could have had plenty of opportunity to attack the girl before that."

"I'm sure he didn't," she said unhappily.

Buchanan shrugged. "What does it matter? The girl wasn't done any permanent harm."

"The villagers are terrified of the vampire threat. They'll

turn on Barnabas if it's proven he could have attacked the girl."

"And you were leaving this note to warn him to establish some kind of alibi?"

"Yes."

"There's no problem. I told you I'm your friend. I'll change my story and say Barnabas was with me most of last evening. That should look after things," Mike said easily.

Carolyn stared at him in amazement "You'd really do that?"

"Why not?"

Swallowing hard, she said, "It may not be necessary."

"If it is, I won't let you down," he promised. "Now I'll slip this note back in your cousin's hands."

Carolyn watched as he carefully inserted the note between the hands of the sleeping Barnabas, wondering whether this were a nightmare, not a reality. It had all the marks of a bad dream.

Mike Buchanan now turned to give her another mocking look. "You thought because I followed you here and criticized your secrecy I meant you harm. You take too much for granted."

"I didn't know," she faltered.

"Now you do," he said, and grasping her by the arm, added, "I think you are right. We should get out of here as soon as possible."

She was in no mood to argue with him, so with a final glance at Barnabas in the casket she allowed the young director to lead her from the chamber of the living dead to the blackness of the main cellar once more. He seemed to make his way along exceedingly well, especially since he wore dark glasses. It was then for the first time that she began to wonder about him and debate whether he might be Quentin Collins, who also bore a curse of the supernatural, come back to Collinwood in the guise of Mike Buchanan. The more she thought about it, the more likely it seemed. She and Barnabas had been suspicious of Jim Swift and all along had ignored the more likely suspect!

They reached the stone steps, and Mike raised one of the wooden cellar doors to allow sunlight and fresh air to flood in on the worn, moss-covered steps. Taking a deep breath, she went on ahead of him up to the level of the grass. He followed her and carefully set down the weatherbeaten wooden door again.

"If we arrange the lock and fittings carefully," he said, "no one will know the door has been broken. We may need this means of entry some time again."

She watched with interest as he worked to arrange the doors and the lock in such a way that the damage was fairly well hidden. At the same time she worried that from now on he would also know of this way of getting into the old house.

She said, "Hurry! Hare could arrive any moment."

Mike stood back and surveyed the doors with satisfaction. "No one will notice unless they try to open the lock, but they probably never use this entrance."

"I wouldn't spend any more time on it."

"No need to," he said, the eyes behind his dark glasses fixed on her. "Now I'll walk you back to Collinwood."

She breathed more easily when they were a distance from the house, but again she found herself wondering if the director could be Quentin Collins. If so, that might explain his interest in Barnabas and the reason he was helping her.

She said, "Why are you so willing to help Barnabas?"

Walking at her side, he answered, "I like him. I also think he's probably a good actor, and he's agreed to appear in several of our shows."

"And what you've discovered now makes no difference?"

"Why should it? By dusk he'll be his old self. No one else need know his secret"

Carolyn gave him a searching look. "You're being very generous."

"Not really," he said. "It could be that one day I'll require a favor from either Barnabas or you. And you'll know you owe it to me."

This served to make her think again that the man walking with her was Quentin. It was the kind of statement you might expect from the other ill-starred member of her family.

She said, "What sort of favor could you want?"

"Who knows?"

She was silent for a moment, then said, "I'd like to meet Quentin. You asked me about him just now, and I couldn't tell you anything at all. I've never seen him."

"Probably he'll turn up one day," Mike said casually.

"I'm sure he will," she agreed. "They say he's as good-looking as Barnabas, but in a different way. And he also has charm. He doesn't want to be a villainous type, but there are times when he can't control the werewolf thing. He changes without wanting to."

"So, like Barnabas, he is something of a martyr?"

"Yes."

They were near the entrance of Collinwood now, and Mike Buchanan halted. "I suggest we forget we ever met this morning. Let's put the whole thing out of our minds."

"I'll be glad to, if you'll agree."

"It's my suggestion," Mike said. "I believe Jim Swift visited you here last night."

"He did."

The director hesitated. "I don't want to alarm you, but I know very little about him. It could be worth your while to go easy with him – at least, until we learn more about his past."

Her eyebrows raised. "Why do you say that?"

"Because he's something of an enigma, and I dislike enigmas. And he seems very intent on winning your friendship. His coming up here on his own last night is an example."

"Is there anything wrong in his wanting to be friends with me?" Carolyn wanted to know.

"No, unless he should happen to be your Quentin Collins."

She listened to his calm statement in silence. It was true she had suspected Jim Swift of being Quentin. So had Barnabas. But that was before this morning. Now she was thinking in different terms, suspecting that Mike could be the elusive Quentin.

With a sigh, she said, "I doubt that he is Quentin."

"But you can't be sure."

"No. I can't be sure."

"Then I'd be on my guard. Just a word of advice. As I keep telling you, I'm on your side," Mike said.

"Why?" she asked.

He smiled bleakly. "There could be any number of reasons. Possibly because I like you, and I want you to like me. Also, you're working for Nicholas Freeze, and you can be useful in helping me borrow some antiques for the shows from him."

"I'm already working on that," she said. "But it would be wise for you to talk to him again."

"I intend to," Mike said, studying her from behind his dark glasses. "It's been an exciting morning."

"Yes."

"When you see Barnabas, tell him not to worry – I'll stand behind him."

"Very well."

Mike smiled. "I think between us we can get your Uncle Roger to ease up on him. That's your goal, isn't it?"

"I suppose so."

"Don't forget you're welcome to come to the theatre at any time," he added. "I'll go back to the cottage now. Jim Swift should be there. He went to the village in my car to bring me out some scripts I want to work on. I left them in the auditorium."

He bade her a casual goodbye and went on his way. She stood watching after him for a long while trying to decide whether he could be Quentin or not. In the end, she knew it was hopeless. She hadn't enough knowledge yet to be sure. She could only await the developments that would tell her.

The rest of the day passed uneventfully. She was careful to keep out of her Uncle Roger's way. In the evening she went up to her own room and began reading. It was a pleasant, warm evening, and she left the window open. As dusk came, she began to wonder and worry about Barnabas. Could anything have happened to him?

tttttttShe had placed her book face down on her lap as it became too dark to read. Now she stared out the window at the blue haze of growing night gradually obscuring her view of the cliffs and the distant ocean. Suddenly from high in the sky there was an eerie screeching cry, and then she saw what seemed like a large bird winging close to the house. In a moment it came bumping against the screen of her window. She rose from her chair with a frightened cry as she realized that this was no bird, but a huge bat!

CHAPTER 5

Carolyn stepped back from the window as the wide-winged creature continued to bump against the screen. And then in a twinkling it had somehow made its way into the room and across to a shadowed corner. As she watched with frightened eyes, Barnabas suddenly emerged from the shadows as calmly assured as ever.

He said, "I hope I didn't frighten you too much. I decided this was my best way of getting in without encountering Roger."

She stared at him with wondering eyes. "I've never seen you do anything like this before."

His smile was bitter. "I only resort to this kind of legerdemain when all else fails."

She went over to her door and locked it so no one could get in and interrupt them. Then she crossed the shadowed room to join him. "Did you get the message I left?" she asked.

"Yes. How did you get down there?"

"Through the cellar entrance," she said, and went on with the details.

Barnabas listened carefully. "Hare will be incensed when he hears how easily you managed to get by him. I've given him orders not to leave the house in the daytime, but sometimes he does wander away."

"I suppose he tires of being shut up alone in the house."

Barnabas nodded. "But that is his responsibility – to guard me when I'm helpless."

Carolyn gave him a worried look. "When I saw you down there like that this morning, I was terribly afraid for you. Especially when Mike Buchanan followed me and learned your secret."

"That was unfortunate."

Carolyn said, "He didn't want me to tell you, but I had no intention of not doing so. Though he seemed friendly and cooperative enough, I've begun to wonder if he isn't Quentin in disguise."

Barnabas reminded her, "We did think Jim Swift might be Quentin."

"I know, and it still is a possibility."

"But the way Mike behaved this morning started giving you other ideas?"

"Yes."

Barnabas looked solemn. "You could be right. I'm not sure that I understand his sudden wish to help me."

"Unless he is Quentin and sympathetic."

"Quentin has opposed me and caused me trouble at times," Barnabas reminded her, "though I haven't blamed him, knowing that he still is under the shadow of that curse."

"He could be trying to make amends."

"If Mike is Quentin," Barnabas agreed. "But it could be that neither Mike nor Jim Swift is Quentin in disguise. He may not be in the village, or he may be lurking here under another identity. The only clue we have that he might be here is that wolf-like phantom you saw in the auditorium. And whoever that was could have gotten in from the street."

"I know that," she said.

"So we really have nothing to go on as yet," Barnabas said grimly. "I'm not sure what Mike Buchanan meant about us being able to do him some favor. We'll have to wait and find out, I suppose."

"I don't really care about Quentin," she said. "I'm worried most about you and the trouble you're in."

"I'll manage," he said.

"Uncle Roger is very angry. He's sure you attacked that girl."

Barnabas's deep-set eyes met hers through the gathering shadows. "Would you be shocked if I told you I am guilty?"

"I think not."

"I am," he said quietly. "I'll be more careful in the future, but I have my needs."

Carolyn, afraid that her face might reflect the shock and horror his words made her feel, was thankful for the shadows. Even though the unfortunate girl had not been harmed, it was frightening to know that Barnabas had been forced to attack her and drain off some of her blood. Carolyn understood he had done this only under duress and that he tried not to harm his victims. She knew that this need of his was as repulsive to him as to her. Only the fact that it stood between him and true death made him continue his vampire ways.

Barnabas understood her silence, saying, "You're disgusted with me."

"No!" she protested.

"Try to understand," he said unhappily.

"I do, but let's not talk about it," she begged.

"Very well," he said. "We'll go on to more pleasant topics. If nothing else complicates matters, I'm going to act in some of the plays."

"Mike told me."

"And you shall come and watch my performances," he said. "None quite as spectacular as the one I've given for you tonight, but I hope to make you and Elizabeth proud of me."

"I know we will be," she said.

"You'll go on working for Nicholas Freeze at the antique barn?"

"Yes."

Barnabas stared out the window. "I've been thinking about that discovery you made. I'm wondering what that miserly Freeze will do with the letter from alchemist John Wykcliffe and the three vessels supposed to contain the life-giving potion."

"I can't guess."

"You'll have a ringside seat to find out," Barnabas said. "His daughter is arriving tomorrow?"

"Yes. Hazel will get here in the morning."

"I'll want to meet her," Barnabas said. "She's staying here, isn't she?"

"Yes."

"Good," Barnabas said. "I'll have plenty of chance to win her friendship. I wonder if she has any idea the sort of man her father is."

"She's visited him occasionally for brief periods," she said. "Hazel has no illusions about him, but she does feel sorry for him."

"I hope her sympathy isn't wasted," Barnabas commented. "Freeze is a hard man. The way he's treated Tom Buzzell and allowed him to sink into drunkenness is an example."

"I know," she agreed.

"Watch yourself," Barnabas cautioned her. "Now that Nicholas Freeze has discovered that potion, there's no telling what weird ideas he may get."

Carolyn stared through the gloom, trying to catch his expression, but couldn't. "What do you mean?"

"I have a premonition of unpleasant happenings at the antique barn," he told her. "I can't tell you anything more definite. I wish you weren't going to be there, but I suppose you can't help it. Hazel is coming, and she'll expect you to work with her."

"We made our plans months ago."

"Then you'll have to carry them through," Barnabas said. "Now I must go."

"When will I see you again?"

"Tomorrow night, if everything goes well."

"You'll get that cellar door repaired?"

"I'll have Hare do it at once," he promised as he came close and held her in his arms for a moment. "Don't fret about me, little cousin. I can manage very nicely."

"You have so many enemies," she said.

"Believe that I'm equal to them," Barnabas said, and he kissed her on the forehead with his icy lips. "Please turn your back to me, and don't look around for a moment."

Carolyn did as she was told, and after she'd stared into a dark corner of the room for several minutes, she wheeled around and he was no longer there. He had vanished swiftly without a sound. It had all been so startling she began to wonder if it had happened at all. Had the scene between them been a figment of her imagination?

She thought not, but she didn't return downstairs, fearing her Uncle Roger or her mother might subject her to a series of embarrassing questions. Instead, she put on the lights and after reading a little longer went to bed early.

When she arrived at the "Olde Antique Barn" the next morning she found a washed-out looking Tom Buzzell beginning his week by repairing the surface of a Sheraton washstand. He studied her with his red-rimmed eyes and said, "I guess I plum forgot about driving you home Friday night."

"You did," she said, with grim amusement. "I hope you're sorry."

He shook his head mournfully. "I'm sorry about everything that happened over the weekend."

"Why do you repeat your mistakes over and over again?" she wanted to know.

Tom Buzzell looked glum as he hesitated over fitting the neat board patch into the stand. "Blame Nicholas Freeze. After I put up with that old skinflint for five days, I've just naturally got to stay drunk the other two."

"You're only hurting yourself."

"Well, miss, there's a certain pleasure at some stages in the suffering," he said, and he went back to work.

She knew there was little use attempting to reform him. Poor Tom was beyond that by a long way.

She went on into the office. Old Nicholas Freeze looked up from his desk to greet her. "You're five minutes late," he said in his reedy voice. "It's five past nine."

"I arrived earlier," she said. "I stopped to speak to Tom a moment."

"I don't pay you to talk nonsense to the other help," Mr. Freeze said in his biting fashion as he got to his feet. "If my daughter is going to work with you, I want you to help set her a good example, and I believe in people being on time."

"Yes, sir," she said.

"I have to go over to Ellsworth and pick up a pair of black Staffordshire china dogs for a customer," he said. "I suppose Hazel will likely arrive while I'm gone."

"Her bus should soon be in," Carolyn agreed.

"Well, you can welcome her," he said, starting out. "Get her started to work as soon as she arrives. We don't have idle hands around here."

"I understand," she said.

At the door, Freeze paused to give her a nasty smile and say, "I hear a girl was attacked on Saturday night. Wouldn't surprise me if your cousin Barnabas knew something about that."

Carolyn pretended to read one of the catalogues and did not answer him. He took the hint and went on out. She gave a sigh of annoyance. He was almost impossible to get along with, and she didn't know how Hazel would ever make out.

She had just started to do some morning dusting when Hazel Freeze arrived, suitcase in hand. Carolyn rushed to greet her and introduce her to Tom Buzzell. Then she took the slim, dark girl and her suitcase into the office.

Hazel glanced around with distaste. "It's not a very neat office, is it?"

"No," Carolyn admitted. "I've done my best but your father seems to prefer it in its present cluttered state."

"Dad is a strange one," Hazel agreed with a smile. "But I'm not going to let anything spoil our summer. We're going to have fun."

"Everyone at Collinwood is looking forward to meeting you," Carolyn told her. "Especially my cousin Barnabas, from England."

"I like Englishmen," Hazel said, her eyes dancing with happy expectancy. "Is he charming?"

"Very."

"Good," she said. "I'd like a flirtation this summer."

"Barnabas is perhaps too old for you," she warned. "But there are some other nice young men in town in the theatre company." And she went into detail about Mike Buchanan and his players.

Afterward she began instructing Hazel in the routine of the antique shop. It developed that the girl knew something about antiques. She was quick to single out some Windsor chairs and Boston rockers. Carolyn took her on a tour of the shadowed, cluttered barn, including the second floor. As they passed the door of the locked area where Nicholas Freeze kept his most valuable items, she again was reminded of the three bottles with the supposed elixir of youth in them, but she didn't say anything to Hazel about her find.

It was close to noon before Nicholas Freeze returned with the items from Ellsworth. Hazel ran to greet the wizened old man who, strangely enough, was her father, though he looked elderly enough to be her grandparent. He greeted her warmly for him and then took her into the office after leaving instructions that they were not to be interrupted.

Outside in the barn itself Tom Buzzell commented to Carolyn, "That's the first time I've ever seen the old man act half human."

"I know," she smiled. "Perhaps having Hazel around will mellow him."

"Don't count on it," was Tom's dour response.

It was fortunate that she didn't, for after being sequestered in the office for an hour with his daughter, Nicholas Freeze returned to his demanding, miserly mood. He ordered them all to work and spent the late afternoon playing cards with his cronies, undertaker William Drape and the alcoholic Dr. Eric Blake.

Hazel didn't seem to mind her father's crotchety nature, and having her around made it much more pleasant for Carolyn. They drove back to Collinwood after work, and she saw her friend settled in a room adjoining hers. Elizabeth unlocked the door between the rooms so they could move back and forth without going into the hall.

The arrival of Hazel at Collinwood put Roger Collins in a better mood. He made no mention of the incident of Saturday night and spent quite a long while explaining the history of the old house to the fascinated Hazel.

Standing in the living room and gazing at the many family portraits, she said, "This is a wonderful house!"

Roger looked pleased. "It has its good points, but all its history is not happy."

"There are few old houses that haven't known some tragedy," Hazel was quick to say.

Elizabeth smiled at her. "I think the good times have far outweighed the bad, as far as I'm concerned."

Hazel said, "I hear that your British cousin Barnabas is visiting here. I'm looking forward to meeting him."

Roger gave Carolyn and her mother an awkward glance and then told their visitor, "No doubt he'll be showing up this evening or some later one. He's pleasant, but rather eccentric."

Hazel lifted her eyebrows. "But Carolyn told me he was charming!"

"He is," Elizabeth said quickly. "With Roger, eccentric and charming mean much the same thing."

It was left until later, when dusk had come, for Barnabas to prove his own qualities. Carolyn and Hazel had deserted the older folk to sit and talk in the garden. Night began to fall, and they still had much to talk about. Suddenly there was a brisk footstep on the gravel walk and Barnabas appeared.

"Good evening," he said in his suave fashion.

Carolyn at once got up and made the introductions. Hazel was obviously impressed by the tall, handsome man. She said, "I've been looking forward to meeting you."

"And I to meeting you," Barnabas said. "Many years ago, I knew your mother."

"Truly?" Hazel was at once excited.

"Yes," Barnabas said. "We saw each other quite a lot. I suppose in the jargon of that day people would have said we were keeping company."

Hazel seemed thrilled. "And what happened?"

Standing there in the growing darkness, Barnabas sighed. "I had to leave the village for a time. I stayed away longer than I intended. When I finally returned, your mother was married to Nicholas Freeze."

"My father is years older than you!" Hazel told him.

"I suppose he seems so," Barnabas acknowledged.

"He is," Hazel insisted. "I wish my mother had married you. I'd much rather have had you as my father."

Barnabas laughed lightly. "Well, suppose I pretend I'm a very close relative. Say, a fond uncle? Then I'll be able to treat you something like a daughter."

Hazel was wistful. "Do I seem that young to you? I was hoping you'd think me nice enough to date."

"I do," Barnabas assured her. "It's only because of knowing your mother I adopt this elderly pose. Otherwise, I'd be enchanted with you as a companion."

Carolyn smiled at her friend. "Be thankful he hasn't decided to sweep you off your feet."

"I haven't made any promises that I mightn't," Barnabas said. After that he asked Carolyn, "How is Roger feeling tonight?"

"In a slightly improved mood. There hasn't been much talk about Saturday night," Carolyn told him.

"Good," Barnabas said, and then changing the subject, added, "I'm going down to see the dress rehearsal of this week's play. They're having it tonight and opening tomorrow evening. Would you girls like to come along?"

"I'd love it," Hazel said at once. "Carolyn told me there are some nice boys in the company."

Barnabas gave Carolyn a reproving glance. "And I thought you were faithful to me!"

"I am," she said, joining in the fun. "That's why I was anxious to have Hazel meet Mike Buchanan and Jim Swift. I didn't want her competing with me for you."

"In that case, you're forgiven," Barnabas said, laughing. "Would you consider driving us to the town hall in your station wagon?"

"I'd be glad to," Carolyn said.

Within a few minutes they were all in the front seat of the battered car, heading for the village. Carolyn had gone into the house for just a moment to tell her mother where they were going and then she came back to lead the others to the car. She was glad that Hazel and Barnabas were getting on so well and looked forward to seeing the rehearsal.

"What play are they doing?" she asked him as she kept busy at the wheel on the winding road.

"*Write Me a Murder*," Barnabas said. "It's an excellent play. I've seen it in both London and New York."

"You must travel a lot," Hazel said, sounding duly impressed.

"Sometimes more than I like," Barnabas told her. He was seated on the outside with Hazel in the middle.

"Barnabas is going to take parts in several of the plays," Carolyn told her friend.

"When?" Hazel asked him.

"I'm starting rehearsals after the performance tomorrow

night," Barnabas said. "We're doing Ibsen's *A Doll's House*. I've played the family-friend role many times, so I'll need a minimum of rehearsals. They've arranged several late evening rehearsals for my benefit, since I can't be with the company during the day."

"Why is that?" Hazel wanted to know.

"I'm busy with other things," Barnabas replied.

At the wheel Carolyn said nothing. She listened to the conversation between the other two as Hazel and Barnabas got to know each other better. At last they reached the parking lot next to City Hall and left the car to go up the stairs to the auditorium. They arrived at an intermission, and the company was scattered between the stage and the main body of the small upstairs theatre.

Mike Buchanan was near the rear of the theatre and came to them with a smile.

"Welcome," he said. "I've been hoping you'd show up."

Carolyn introduced Hazel. The director seemed interested in her. Barnabas went down to the stage to talk with some of the other members of the company while Mike went into a description of the play for Hazel's benefit.

Carolyn wandered off by herself to study the stage setting from the other side of the small auditorium. While she was doing this, someone came up beside her and touched her arm. She turned and faced Jim Swift. "Well," he said. "We meet again."

"The last I saw of you was when you walked off into the night," she said. "You didn't get wet on your way to the cottage, did you?"

"No. Most of the rain had stopped," the young actor said. "I'm glad."

"And I enjoyed my visit to your spooky old house."

She smiled at him. "You seemed so at home I was sure you'd been there before."

"Just my easy actor's way," he told her. Nodding in the direction of Hazel, who was talking to Mike Buchanan at the other side of the auditorium, he said, "Mike seems to be hitting it off well with your attractive girl friend."

"He does," she agreed. "Her name is Hazel Freeze. She's the daughter of the man who runs the antique shop where I'm working."

Jim looked surprised. "Old Nicholas Freeze?"

"She's the child of his old age."

"She'd have to be," Jim said, with some amazement. "And she's pretty. Doesn't look like him at all."

"They say she's very like her mother."

"Then she must have been a beauty," Jim said. "I'll have to meet her later."

"She's a nice girl."

"Mike apparently thinks so. You'd better watch him," Jim warned. "He can be a smoothie with the girls."

Carolyn gave him an amused look. "Worse than you?"

He looked hurt. "I'm not that type. I'm very sincere."

"I wonder," she said.

"Give yourself a chance to know me better, and you'll see," he said. "You're always getting rid of me."

"I didn't realize that."

He eyed her wryly. "I think you somehow associate me with that monster you claim you saw here in the auditorium the first night we met."

"I did see a man with a wolf's face."

"And in the back of your mind you believe it was me."

"I don't think so."

"But you're not sure," he said quickly. "It's your subconscious that has me down for a villain."

"Probably. I'm still not able to make up my mind about you," she smiled at him.

"Just what I said."

Carolyn thought that if he were Quentin he was playing his role of the innocent very smoothly. She glanced across to where Mike Buchanan was talking with Hazel. Now, for the first time, she realized that the director was much older than she'd judged him to be. She noticed the deep lines showing in his face and a slight hint of jowls. Again it struck her that he was a much more likely type to be Quentin than the young actor at her side.

At this point Mike left Hazel and called out, "Places, please, for the second act."

"My cue," Jim said. "I'll see you after rehearsal."

Carolyn and Hazel sat at the back of the auditorium and watched the second act of the mystery play. Barnabas had taken a seat by himself a few rows ahead of them. Mike Buchanan sat in the front of the theatre as the play went on. The performances were good, and Carolyn was impressed by the competence of Jim Swift's acting in the role of the older brother in the mystery.

The company went on with the third act without a break. Mike Buchanan gave the actors a few tips from notes he had made, and then the company was dismissed. Carolyn, Hazel, and Barnabas congratulated the director afterward, and he seemed pleased.

"We'll be expecting you for rehearsal after the performance tomorrow night," he informed Barnabas.

"I'll be here," Barnabas said.

Mike turned to Hazel. "I've enjoyed meeting you. Come

here whenever you like. I hope we'll have a chance to see each other when I have more time."

"I'd like that," she said. "I hear you're going to get some antiques from my father's shop for the stage settings."

"I'm coming by to talk to him about that tomorrow," Mike said. "Maybe I'll see you then."

"I'll be there, working along with Carolyn," Hazel said with a smile.

Mike turned to Carolyn and with a meaningful expression said, "It was a most interesting weekend, wasn't it?"

Knowing this was a veiled reference to their experiences at the old house Sunday morning, she murmured; "Yes, it was."

They said their goodnights, and she left without seeing Jim Swift again. The young actor must still have been backstage. She was slightly nervous about the way Mike Buchanan had made it a point to remind her he'd not forgotten about Barnabas. She wondered if he would use his knowledge as a threat over her. It was an upsetting thought.

They drove back to Collinwood with Barnabas entertaining Hazel with stories about his adventures in the theatre. Once in a long while Carolyn would join in the conversation, but for the most part she drove in worried silence. At the door of Collinwood Barnabas said goodnight, and they went inside.

When they had changed for bed, Hazel came into Carolyn's room for a few minutes and sat on the edge of her bed in her nightgown. "I had a marvelous time," she enthused. "I think Barnabas is terrific."

"I thought you would," she smiled.

"And Mike is extremely interesting."

"A very keen young man," Carolyn said. "But he may also be a bit shallow. I wouldn't depend on what he says too much. Theatre people are great deceivers."

Hazel sounded surprised. "Do you mean that?"

"I'm afraid so. I like Jim Swift, the young man I was talking to, but I'm not sure I believe everything he tells me."

"But that's terrible!" Hazel wailed. "I think people should be honest above everything else."

"It seemed I should warn you," Carolyn said, as she mentally asked herself what her girl friend would think if she knew the charming Barnabas was a vampire and either of the other two men could be the werewolf-cursed Quentin in disguise. Better to save that shattering revelation until later – Hazel had absorbed enough surprises for one evening.

The girls said goodnight. Hazel asked if she might leave the door between their rooms open for company. Carolyn willingly agreed. They turned off their lights, and Carolyn soon sank into a deep sleep. But it was not to last through the night.

She awoke to darkness with a strange sensation of fear. A conviction that something sinister had happened had awakened her. Thinking of her friend asleep in the next room, she sat up in bed quietly, not wanting to make any needless noise. But the feeling of danger persisted. There was an eerie sensation of a supernatural evil that she could not ignore. She wanted to scream out, but didn't dare!

CHAPTER 6

The presence of a threatening phantom lurking in the shadows of the bedroom was so real for Carolyn that she felt it might suddenly reach out bony fingers and grasp her. She could no longer restrain herself. In spite of not wanting to cause her friend in the other room undue alarm, she uttered a frantic scream.

She expected to hear some response from Hazel at once, but there was none, and now her fear grew worse. Trembling, she stared into the darkness, wondering why Hazel hadn't heard her and answered.

She called out her friend's name. "Hazel!"

There was no reply, and now concern for Hazel outweighed her fears. She scrambled from the bed and ran toward the open door to her friend's room. Again she called out her name, and again there was no answer. Frantically she groped for the wall switch to turn on the ceiling light in Hazel's bedroom. She finally found it and snapped it on.

The light revealed Hazel's bed rumpled and empty! Carolyn stared at the empty bed in dismay. What did it mean? What had happened to the other girl? Had the evil that had curdled her blood been actually threatening Hazel? Where had she gone?

Carolyn tried the bathroom that served both rooms, and it, too, was empty. Hazel had definitely left the suite. Now, almost without thinking, she moved to the window and gazed out. It was a moonlit night, and down in the gardens she saw a startling tableau. Hazel, in her flowing white nightgown, in the arms of Barnabas. At that distance she couldn't be sure, but it seemed to her that Barnabas had his lips pressed to the throat of the pretty girl!

Carolyn watched with a shocked expression. Some of her fear left her. She knew now it had been Hazel leaving the room which had wakened her. Her friend would be fairly safe, even though Barnabas would take blood from her. It was a means of getting his needs for the night fulfilled without venturing into the village and risking further scandal. She could understand the extremity of his position, but she still was upset that he should have chosen Hazel for his victim.

As she watched, he let Hazel go. The dark-haired girl stood staring up at him for a few seconds and then turned and began walking back toward the house. She moved slowly like someone in a dream. It was apparent to Carolyn that Barnabas had used his hypnotic powers to induce the girl to come to him in a sleepwalking state. No doubt the spell would suffice to bring her safely back to bed.

Knowing it might be disastrous to wake her up, Carolyn quickly turned off the bright light in her friend's room and retreated to her own bedroom once more. There she turned on a small night light and sat on the bed waiting for Hazel to appear. It took quite a few minutes. Then the door of the other room was slowly opened and closed. Seconds later, Hazel floated across to her bed and like an automaton sat down and then stretched out and drew the bedclothes over her. She seemed safely asleep once more. Carolyn kept a silent vigil for some time before she wearily turned off the night light and returned to bed.

She almost had forgotten the incident by the next morning, but Hazel brought it to mind as they started down the stairs to breakfast. "I had a lot of the weirdest dreams last night," her friend said.

"Being in a strange room and bed," Carolyn suggested.

Her friend hesitated on the stairs. "Strange rooms haven't acted on me like that before."

"Too much excitement."

"Likely," the other girl agreed. She gave her a wan smile. "I had this nightmare about walking in the garden with Barnabas. It still seems real to me."

"Barnabas really did make an impression on you," Carolyn said, trying to keep it on a light level so her friend wouldn't guess what had happened. At the same time she glanced quickly at Hazel's throat and saw the betraying red mark there.

"Don't you dare tell him," Hazel said. "He'd tease me about it."

"I'll not say anything," she promised. And then she asked, "Did all that dreaming make you feel ill?"

"No. I feel fine," the dark-haired girl said. "So I shouldn't complain. I'll be used to the new surroundings by tonight."

They had breakfast and drove to the village and the antique shop. The summer visitors had begun to stream into Collinsport and so the girls had a busy day. Nicholas Freeze was in a beaming mood as he managed to sell a copper rooster weathervane that he'd had in stock for months. Carolyn found a customer for a Victorian slant-lid desk. Hazel, who was looking after several counters of smaller items in the shadowed barn, sold a number of antique bottles, including a Success to Railroad flask and a Cathedral bottle.

True to his word, Mike Buchanan arrived in the afternoon to see about stage furnishings for the Ibsen play. Nicholas Freeze was in such a good frame of mind he agreed to let the company have the use of a lot of Victorian furniture.

Mike talked with Hazel for a while and then managed to seek out Carolyn privately in a dark corner of the barn. "I've enjoyed meeting Hazel," he told her.

Carolyn said, "She's a nice girl."

"What about that red mark on her throat?" he asked in a knowing tone.

She felt herself go pale. "What do you mean?"

"You know," he said. "It's the mark left by Barnabas. She isn't even aware it's there."

"You must be wrong!"

"I don't think so," he said evenly. "Is that any way to treat a friend? Turn her over to a vampire!"

"I haven't done that!"

Mike Buchanan was grim. "He's gotten at her somehow."

"You have to be wrong!" she protested weakly.

"I know that I'm not," Mike Buchanan said, "and I want you to make sure it doesn't happen again."

"How can I?"

"You can talk to Barnabas," the director said. "And if he won't listen, let him know that I'm on to what is happening. And if he continues with it, I'll cause him some problems."

"Tell him yourself."

"No, I prefer to have you do it," Mike said. "It will be better that way."

After he left, Carolyn stood in the cool shadows of the barn, surrounded by the dusty antiques of countless years and trembling at the threat just offered by the young stage director. She doubted that Barnabas would admit to what he'd done, or if he did, whether he'd promise not to repeat his crime.

Before they left that evening, Nicholas Freeze summoned Hazel to his office for a private conversation with him, and when Hazel got into the car with Carolyn for the drive home, she seemed badly worried.

As they drove along, Carolyn asked, "Did your father say something to upset you?"

Hazel gave her a troubled glance. "Do you think he's quite right in his mind?"

It was a touchy question. Carolyn hesitated over it as she went on driving. Then she finally said, "I don't think he's actually demented, but he is rather strange. I suppose eccentric would be the best description for him."

"I agree," Hazel said.

"What makes you ask?"

"Something he said to me in the office just now."

"Oh?" She didn't want to press her friend for any personal information, so she left it at that.

After a moment Hazel said, "You know that he found those bottles with some kind of strange potion in them?"

"John Wykcliffe's elixir of youth. I made the discovery by accident."

"The bottles are very old, aren't they?"

"Centuries old," Carolyn said from the wheel.

"Do you really think that old chemist found a liquid that can give eternal youth?"

"No. He may have discovered some health-giving medicine, but I don't think there is any such thing as an elixir of youth."

"My father does. He believes those three bottles hold enough of the precious stuff to extend the lives of dozens of people. He thinks he'll make a fortune from it."

"Trust him to think of the money side," Carolyn said with a bitter, amused look. "The liquid is likely worthless."

"He considers it precious, and he's after me to be the first to try it," Hazel said bleakly.

Carolyn gave her a worried glance. "Did he actually say that?"

"Yes. He began the other day, and he asked me again tonight. He says Dr. Blake will give it to me by hypodermic, and I won't even notice it."

"Don't let him. Dr. Blake is a crazy old alcoholic. I wouldn't trust him to treat me, and I surely wouldn't let him inject something into my veins that might hurt me."

"Father claims he has read all the journals of John Wykcliffe and knows all about the potion."

"I read a letter that was with the three bottles, and it warned that the liquid could be dangerous under certain conditions,"

Carolyn told her. "Tell your father you're not interested."

"I will," she said nervously. "I'm not sure he'll listen."

"Above all, don't let him talk you into any experiments," Carolyn warned her.

They had reached Collinwood by this time, so nothing more was said of the elixir, but it went on bothering Carolyn. Because she had been the one who'd first discovered the dust-covered bottles, she felt a responsibility concerning them. She wasn't surprised that the miserly old Nicholas Freeze wanted to sell the youth potion for a ridiculous profit, but she was shocked that he had chosen his daughter as the first one to be given the ancient potion.

Perhaps in his twisted mind he considered this as a special gift for her. He wished to preserve her present loveliness forever, but he wasn't thinking of the possible dangers to which he was exposing this only child of his old age. Hazel would have to be somehow protected from his misguided schemes.

Along with this worry was her concern about Barnabas preying on the girl. The warning given her by Mike Buchanan had thoroughly upset her. She had not intended to say anything. If Hazel felt no ill results of Barnabas's taking some of her blood nightly and it enabled him to survive, she was willing to close her eyes to it until he found some other solution to his dilemma. But with the threat from Mike everything had changed. Now she must seek out Barnabas alone and try to reason with him.

After dinner while Hazel and Roger were talking she quietly slipped out of the main house and took the path to the older mansion where Barnabas was living. It was dusk by the time she reached the door and used the rapper. After a moment the door was opened by the coarse-faced Hare. He thrust his beard-stubbled face out at her and uttered one of his low growls.

"Where is your master?" she asked.

Glaring at her, he pointed toward the field.

"He's gone down there?"

Hare nodded, continued to glare at her a moment longer, and then slammed the door closed in her face. With a sigh she turned and went down the steps. Now she headed across the field and down the slope that led to the family cemetery. She guessed that she might find Barnabas there. She knew it was one of his favorite haunts.

Though dusk was slowly settling, it was still far from dark. She reached the gates of the cemetery and went inside with some feelings of uneasiness. She always felt nervous in this silent world of the dead. Picking her way between the rows of gravestones, she kept searching for Barnabas. At last she spied him standing before a weathered gray headstone.

He also saw her as she came up to him. He turned from the

grave by which he'd been standing and said, "What brought you down here?"

"I had to see you."

"But I was going to visit the house after I left here."

"I had to talk to you alone," she said urgently.

A frown crossed his handsome face. "What is wrong now?"

"Everything," she said unhappily. "Mike knows that you've been taking Hazel's blood. Don't deny it, because I saw you from the window."

"I've not harmed her."

"Mike doesn't believe that."

"What does he know about it?" Barnabas asked with some anger.

She gave him a pleading look. "He knows about you and what you are! And he told me to warn you about touching Hazel again."

"And if I ignore his warning?"

"I don't know what he'll do. Tell the police, I suppose."

"He has no right to interfere," Barnabas said angrily. "I only mean to turn to Hazel for a few nights. I have a plan. Why does he want to spoil it?"

"He's jealous of you and your power over Hazel," she said. "I think Mike is really Quentin in disguise."

"In that case, Hazel could be in danger from him," Barnabas said bitterly.

"Not if he loves her."

"Even if he loves her," Barnabas asserted. "When the werewolf curse descends on him he has little power to fight it. He could commit some terrible act and not even remember it."

"You're sure?"

"I know more about it than anyone," Barnabas warned her.

She gave him a despairing look. "What can we do?"

He stood there grimly. "I'll have to think about it. In the meantime I'm due at a rehearsal after the performance tonight, and I'll have to accept Mike Buchanan for what he is, the director of the company. I'll not even be able to hint that I believe he is Quentin."

"It will give you a chance to observe him closely and decide whether he really is Quentin or not."

"It won't be easy to tell."

"I think you'd better not put Hazel under another spell until all this is settled," she said.

Barnabas's handsome face was a study in perplexity. At last he said, "Very well. If you ask it, I'll manage."

"You can have my blood, Barnabas," she said gently. "I want to help you."

He shook his head. "No. You're too close to me. I don't want that. I'll find someone else."

"Who?"

"Does it matter? Let me worry about that. You can tell Mike Buchanan you gave me his message and I've agreed to keep away from Hazel."

"That's not all," she said.

"What else?"

She went on to tell him about Nicholas Freeze and his insane plan to give Hazel the supposed elixir of life. She ended with, "I can see that he may feel he's being kind to her in trying to keep her perpetually young, but I think the liquid is worthless and possibly dangerous."

"She mustn't let that crazy old man try anything of the sort," Barnabas said.

"I've already told her that."

"Does she see how wrong it all is?"

"Yes, but she is being nagged by her father, and she seems to have a kind of awe of him."

Barnabas frowned. "I'll try and talk to her about it."

"I wish you would."

"Perhaps before the rehearsal tonight," he said. "I'll go back to Collinwood with you now."

"She's there talking to Roger," Carolyn told him.

"I'll have to wait my chance for a few words alone with her," Barnabas said. Taking her by the arm, he began leading her out of the cemetery. "Let us hurry."

Carolyn wasn't sure whether Barnabas managed his few words with Hazel alone or not. Roger kept talking until late and then Barnabas was forced to leave for the rehearsal. Hazel complained of being tired, and so they went to bed as soon as Barnabas left. Carolyn thought it best not to query her friend about what Barnabas had said, and Hazel volunteered no information.

The next day proved another busy one. During her lunch hour Carolyn went to do some personal shopping on the main street. Hazel remained behind to help at the antique barn, and planned to take her lunch period an hour later. Carolyn was just coming out of the women's wear store with some stockings when she almost bumped into Jim Swift.

Jim said, "This is a coincidence. I've been thinking about you."

"That's too familiar a story for me to believe," she told him.

"I mean it," he said. "You weren't at the rehearsal last night."

"No."

"You should have been there. Mike was in one of his irritable moods. I thought for a while he and Barnabas were going to have a quarrel, but they finally settled their differences and the rehearsal went along fine."

"I'm glad of that," she said with relief. Jim Swift didn't know that the antagonism between Mike and Barnabas was over Hazel. Better that he didn't.

Jim said, "Where can we go and have coffee together?"

"I've just finished lunch," she protested.

He smiled at her. "You could stand an extra coffee."

She sighed. "Well, there's the hotel lunchroom."

"Good idea," he said. "We'll go there." He took her by the arm and started in the direction of the hotel.

Within a few minutes she was sitting across from him at one of the tables that looked out onto the main street through murky picture windows. Their steaming coffees were on the table before them.

"I can't stay long," she warned him.

"I just want to talk to you for a few minutes," he said.

"Well, then?"

Jim was studying her closely. "Are you in love with Barnabas?" he asked bluntly.

She crimsoned. "Why do you ask that?"

"I want to know. Because I'm in love with you."

She shook her head. "Nonsense!"

"I mean it," he said seriously. "I haven't much to offer, I admit that. But I'm not sure about this Barnabas, either. He's so eccentric that I can't see him as being good for you. He's a kind of relative of yours, isn't he?"

"I'm very fond of Barnabas," she told him. "But I've never considered him as someone I might marry."

Jim Swift's young face showed relief. "That's good news."

She smiled ruefully. "I'm not saying I mightn't change my mind, if he gave me any encouragement."

"He won't," Jim said.

She was surprised. "You sound very sure of that!"

"It's just a hunch."

She sipped her coffee. "You're a strange person."

"Aren't all actors a little weird? Even your Barnabas? Incidentally, he's excellent in this Ibsen play."

"I expected he would be."

"Mike had to grudgingly give him some praise after the rehearsal, but I could tell that it really hurt him to do it."

"What kind of a person is Mike Buchanan?"

Jim stared down at his coffee. "This is my first time working with him, but I'd call him complex, hard to understand – but a good director. And by the way, he's smitten with that Hazel."

"Honestly?"

"You bet," Jim said. "I can tell. Mike has fallen for her hard."

"I'm not sure she likes him all that much," Carolyn said. "She has a kind of crush on Barnabas."

Jim smiled wryly. "Don't all you girls?"

"The way I feel about him isn't exactly like having a crush. It goes much deeper."

"He charms every female around," Jim told her with a twinkle in his brown eyes. "I'll be satisfied if I wind up with you."

"Is that the important thing you had to tell me?"

"It's important to me," he insisted.

She sipped some more of the hot coffee. "Do you think there is any mystery to Mike Buchanan?"

"Mystery?" Jim sounded puzzled.

"What I mean is, could he be using a false name? Could he be someone else pretending to be Mike Buchanan?"

Jim's eyebrows raised. "Where did you get that wild idea?"

She sighed and decided to confide in him. "I have a reason."

"Tell me."

She still hesitated. Then, looking at the actor with serious eyes, she said, "There is a member of the Collins family who occasionally comes back here in some disguise. He's very clever at it, and most times he's not recognized."

"Why does he have to do this?"

"Some years ago he got in serious trouble, and he's been in trouble several times since. I'm not going into the kind of trouble," she said, "but my family has been very much worried by him."

"And you think Mike might be this fellow?"

"Yes," she said. "His name is Quentin... Quentin Collins. I've been wondering if Mike isn't Quentin."

"That's a new one," Jim said, seeming astounded.

"You've never heard him mention that name?"

"No."

"It's not likely he would," she said with a deep sigh. "If he is Quentin, he might cause all of us trouble. Or he might not. He isn't really a bad person but he suffers from a condition that makes his actions unpredictable."

"Mike can be unpredictable."

"But not in the way I mean," she said. "At least I think not."

Jim Swift looked baffled. "You've told me a lot, and yet you haven't really told me much," he said. "What you're asking me to do is watch Mike and see if I can find anything about him to link him to this Quentin Collins."

"If you will."

"I'll do almost anything for you," he said. "Does this give me a lead ahead of Barnabas?"

She smiled. "It means you're my friend."

"At least that's a beginning."

"You don't have to do it if you don't want to," she said.

"I'll do it," he assured her. "But I doubt if it will lead to anything. I say Mike is on the level. At least, I mean he's himself. I also happen to figure he can be a tricky guy. But that's another story."

"I'll be relieved knowing you're helping," she said.

Jim Swift gave her a reassuring grin. "Our romance is finally getting under way," he said happily.

He walked her back to the "Olde Antique Barn" and she returned to work. She'd enjoyed her chat with Jim and felt she had at least one friend in the company who would spy on Mike for her. She couldn't imagine why she'd suspected Jim of being Quentin in the beginning. It had been foolishness on her part. She'd missed the fact that Mike Buchanan was the one most likely to be her troublesome distant cousin.

She would tell Barnabas about her conversation with the actor when she saw him in the evening. The thought of Barnabas brought a slight chill to her. She pictured that coffin in the shadowed room and the face that stared up at her from it, the sallow, wax like face of one of the dead. Barnabas would be in his casket at this very moment looking exactly as he had when she'd first seen him there. She tried to dismiss the memory without too much success.

Hazel had gone into her father's office to have her lunch. Since there were no customers, Carolyn went up to the second floor to do some dusting. She found the alcoholic Tom Buzzell up there polishing a big mirror with an ornate frame.

"Boss sold this while you were out," he informed Carolyn with a sly grin. "For about twice what it's worth."

"He seems to do that most of the time," she said.

"Yep. He has a way with him in spite of being such a miserable critter," Tom said, busy at the mirror. "Wonder why the Doc is here so early in the day."

"The Doc?"

"You know," Tom said, "Doc Blake. He comes here every day for a card game. But he's here early today, and Bill Drape ain't with him. He came in a little while ago totin' that doctor's little black bag, and old Nicholas took him right into the office."

"Is he still here?"

"I reckon so," Tom said, halting to study the mirror before continuing his polishing job.

"Hazel is in the office now having her lunch. Both her father and the doctor must be in there with her."

"Either one of them would be enough to spoil my appetite," Tom commented. "Both of them would be plumb fatal."

Carolyn was becoming increasingly agitated. She didn't like it at all. She had that feeling of sinister evil closing in on her again – an evil she couldn't strike out at. What obscene thing were Nicholas Freeze and the doctor planning? Was Hazel in danger at this moment?

The thought terrified her so that she abruptly turned to go back down and enter the office. Tom Buzzell saw her leaving and called out, "What's the matter?"

"I'll tell you later," she said over her shoulder and hurried for the rough plank stairway. All she could think of now was Hazel and her safety.

Hurrying down the stairway she started along the length of the cluttered, dark barn to the office. She was breathless as she came near the door. But as she headed toward the office, Mike Buchanan suddenly entered the barn and came quickly to block her way.

"I want to talk to you," he said.

"I can't now," she protested. "I have to go into the office."

"Don't try that trick on me," he said angrily, still standing in her way.

"Please!" she begged, trying to get by him as she pictured Hazel in danger from her father and the quack doctor. She couldn't forget the madness they'd tried to urge on the hapless girl.

"I want to talk to you about Hazel," Mike argued, still blocking her path.

"It's because of Hazel I want to go into the office," she almost screamed at him. "She may be in some kind of terrible danger! Please let me by!"

CHAPTER 7

The intensity of her words finally got through to him, and with a startled expression on his tanned face, Mike Buchanan at last stepped aside and let her pass. She ran to the office door, and quickly opening it, went inside. At the rear of the office Nicholas Freeze was standing watching while the elderly Dr. Blake injected something into Hazel's bare upper arm with a hypodermic needle.

Carolyn rushed over to the group and demanded, "What is going on here?"

Hazel gazed at her with a look of frantic appeal. "Please! It's all right," she said.

Nicholas Freeze showed a scowl on his mean, wrinkled face and demanded, "What right have you to come in here asking such questions?"

Hazel glanced at her father. "Please don't be upset. She's only trying to protect me."

Nicholas Freeze was angry. "Hazel is my flesh and blood. She doesn't need protection from anything that happens here."

The decrepit Dr. Blake finished the injection and turned to Carolyn with the hypodermic still in his trembling hand. "Perhaps I can satisfy your worries, young lady. I have found Miss Freeze to be suffering from a mild anemia, and I have administered a suitable tonic by needle."

Hazel nodded. "That is true, Carolyn. Dr. Blake proposes to give me a series of such liver injections to improve my blood. He wants me in a healthy state for an experiment he'd like me to help him with later on." Carolyn listened to this in a somewhat stunned state, and she began to understand. Hazel had given her the hint. The dark-haired girl had agreed to the liver shots since they couldn't do her any harm. Later, she would either postpone taking the elixir her father was forcing on her or refuse to have any part in his proposed experiment.

Nicholas Freeze gave her a scornful look. "Now do you understand?"

"Yes," she said. "I'm sorry I interrupted you."

The two elderly men and the young girl seated in the chair made a strange tableau. Carolyn had a desire to rush out of the dingy office and away from her embarrassment.

Hazel said, "I'll see you in a moment."

"Yes," she replied awkwardly. "I'll be outside."

She turned and hurried from the office closing the door after her and found Mike Buchanan waiting for her in the cool shadows of the barn.

"What was that all about?" he asked.

"Nothing. I had a scare."

He wasn't satisfied. "You said it had something to do with Hazel."

"I thought she was in danger. She's all right."

"What sort of danger?"

"It's not important," she said, wishing he'd go.

He gave her a hard look. "I don't much like mysteries."

"I'm sorry."

"I hope this hasn't anything to do with Barnabas or his preying on her," the young man said.

"It hasn't."

"You gave him my message."

"Yes. He promised me he wouldn't bother her again."

"I guess he kept his promise," Mike said with a wise smile. "Last night one of the girls from the hippie colony was attacked. It's the second time it has happened."

"I'd rather not hear about it," she said faintly.

"No harm done," Mike said. "Except maybe to the reputation of Barnabas. The girl was in the usual daze, but she remembered someone in a caped coat coming out of the night at her. After that, blank – and of course the red dot on her throat."

"Why are you so interested?" she asked, wondering once again if he were really Quentin.

"I know suspicion will eventually get around to Barnabas,

and I don't want to lose the services of a good actor. Too bad he has that problem." He glanced toward the closed office door. "I guess it's no use my waiting to see Hazel. She's going to be in there for some time?"

"I don't know."

"Tell her I was asking for her," Mike Buchanan said. "And the next time you decide to have hysterics, I'd like you to tell me the reason. I'll let it pass this once." With a derisive smile he left the barn and went out the drive to the sunshine.

Carolyn returned to her work with a peculiar feeling of tension. The talk with Mike had not been pleasant, nor had her awkward entrance into the office been received too well. And now on top of all this there had come the disturbing word that Barnabas had sought out one of the hippie crowd again to satisfy his nocturnal need.

In offering him her own blood she had hoped to save him from going out into the village for victims, but he'd refused her. Perhaps he had some hope that one day he'd be cured of the curse, and he wanted no dark shadows of his past between them. She had never seen him in his vampire role. With her he had always been the kind, thoughtful gentleman.

A woman from the summer colony came in search of paintings. Carolyn showed her some primitive oils and a watercolor by Waters. The woman was hard to please and looked at paintings by Allport, Spade, and Grammer before selecting a pastoral scene. By the time she left, Hazel had returned to work.

Hazel came over to the counter of fine cut glass which Carolyn was arranging more neatly and said, "Thank you for the courageous way you came to my aid in the office."

Carolyn gave her a bleak look. "And it turned out you didn't need my help after all."

"The important thing was you were there to defend me!"

"From liver injections," she said, making grim humor of it. "I guess old Dr. Blake is capable of giving them to you."

Hazel, though pale, looked wistfully amused. "He seemed nice enough. He insists I take them every day this week."

She lifted her eyebrows. "Is your blood down that much?"

"So he says. And I don't imagine it can do me any harm."

Carolyn's eyes met hers. "But later they'll expect you to go through with that experiment. At least from what you said."

"I guessed you'd know I was saying that for their benefit," Hazel told her. "I have no thought of taking that potion of youth or elixir of life, or whatever my father calls it."

"You shouldn't," Carolyn warned her.

"I don't intend to. When the liver shots are ended, I'll find some excuse. Father can rant and rave, but he can't make me take that potion against my will."

"I was afraid that was what was going on when I went into the office," she explained. "Tom Buzzell told me Dr. Blake was here – and there had to be a reason."

"So now you know," Hazel said with a smile.

"And it's a relief," she acknowledged.

That night Carolyn waited at the house to talk to Barnabas, but he didn't show up. She knew he had to be at the rehearsal after the show, but she didn't want to go into town that late. Hazel seemed weary and had mentioned going to bed early, so it seemed she would just have to miss seeing the handsome Britisher and telling him what had gone on. Her main worry was that he would again involve himself in trouble by seeking out one of the village girls or some of the hippie crowd for another attack.

The danger of this was underlined when her Uncle Roger sought her out in the living room under the painting of Angelique. There was a troubled frown on his face.

"No sign of Barnabas tonight?" he asked.

"Not so far."

He consulted his wristwatch. "It's nearly ten o'clock. Since he isn't here now, it isn't likely he will come."

"Perhaps not," she said.

Roger gave a deep sigh. "I had something I wanted to tell him."

"He'll be in the village for after the show. They're having a late rehearsal when the regular performance ends."

Roger's brows met in annoyance. "I'm not going to run in there at that late hour to see him."

She said, "I just wanted to let you know where he would be."

"I hope he doesn't behave rashly again," Roger worried. "There was another incident last night."

She pretended innocence. "No one told me."

"Another of the hippie crowd was attacked."

"And they blame Barnabas?"

"No outright accusations have been made," Roger said irritably. "But an officer from the State Police called at my office this afternoon asking me a lot of questions about our British cousin."

A chill of fear pierced her. "Did he say whether it had anything to do with the attacks?"

"He mentioned the rumor that Barnabas had been mixed up in something like this before."

"So you think they are watching him? Perhaps waiting to make a charge against him?"

"It's very likely."

Carolyn looked up at the painting of the black-haired, lovely Angelique. "What a lot of trouble she created with that curse of hers!"

Roger regarded the portrait of the arrogant, long-ago beauty with some disdain. "She cast a blight on the Collins name from which we've never recovered. Elizabeth should remove the painting from here."

"I wouldn't go that far. It is a very fine work of art."

"The subject revolts me," her uncle said. And turning to her again, he added, "By the way, that police officer also mentioned Quentin."

"Indeed? Why?"

"He wanted to know if we'd heard from him lately."

"What did you tell him?"

"I explained that the family and Quentin were not on the best of terms, and that should he come back here it is very unlikely he'd let us know."

"Which is true."

"Unfortunately," Roger said with a hint of despair in his voice, "the Collins name has suffered more from Barnabas and Quentin than from any other source."

"Yet Barnabas is a very pleasant person, and many people claim that Quentin is equally likable."

"Until you cross them," Roger said irritably. "Then they are different altogether. I know."

Carolyn smiled sadly. "Poor Uncle Roger. You have to take the brunt of all the family problems."

"I do," he agreed. "I'm sure Elizabeth is secretly sympathetic to those two. She always welcomes Barnabas when he comes here. She closes her eyes to the dual side of their natures."

"It could be the best way," she suggested.

"Not from my point of view," Roger replied stiffly.

Carolyn's sleep was troubled that night. She worried about not seeing Barnabas and the news that the police were almost at the point of charging him with the attacks on the village girls. She speculated on how he'd made out at the rehearsals and whether the director was really Quentin playing a new role. At last she went to sleep.

But she wakened several times before morning. Each time she was alarmed by the restless sounds from the other bedroom. Through the open door she could hear Hazel tossing and moaning in her bed. It frightened Carolyn, and she worried that Barnabas still might have a spell cast over her.

It was raining the next day, making the barn antique shop seem even more dismal than usual. Nicholas Freeze sent his daughter to the bank in mid-morning and then joined Carolyn in the main area of the shadowed barn.

The rain on the roofs weathered shingles made a loud background of pattering.

Carolyn had the weird feeling that her crotchety boss was trying to be unusually friendly with her. She was polishing a rare signed Tiffany lamp when he came to stand by her, a sly smile on his wrinkled face.

"You're doing very well," he said. "I'm glad I hired you."

"Thank you," she said.

He peered at her in the shadowed gloom. "And you're a good friend of my daughter. You and your mother have been very kind to Hazel."

"We like her."

He nodded. "Yes. I'm sure of that. Thinking it over, I can appreciate why you burst into the office yesterday as you did. It was in Hazel's best interests, and I can't complain about that."

It was a touchy subject and Carolyn said quietly, "I didn't know what Dr. Blake had planned."

"You were quite right to inquire," he said smoothly, as he stood there cracking his lean knuckles. "Quite right!"

She lifted up a small but fine cloisonné vase to divert his attention. "This is a lovely item," she said.

"Excellent," he agreed. "You have good taste. Match it with good judgment and you'll go far."

There was the uncomfortable hint in his words that she should cooperate with him and tolerate his weird ideas. Knowing that he was still planning to have his daughter be the guinea pig for the ancient potion, she had no wish to encourage him into believing she might line up on his side.

She asked him some questions about a fine cherry grandfather's clock with inlay bracket base, fretwork on the bonnet, and brass works. It was purely a diversionary measure, but it served to turn the conversation into a different channel, and Mr. Freeze's eyes lit up as he described the merits of the antique clock.

Later in the afternoon Dr. Blake arrived, and before the ritual card game between Freeze, the doctor, and undertaker William Drape began, the doctor gave Hazel her injection.

It was that evening when Hazel first complained of the headaches that were to continue tormenting her. Almost as soon as she left the dinner table, she went up to her room. Roger had gone back to the village to his office, so Carolyn and her mother were left alone downstairs.

"I wonder what gave Hazel the headache." Elizabeth sounded troubled.

"I don't know," Carolyn said. "I'm worried about those liver treatments she's taking. They could be too strong for her. Dr. Blake is not really responsible these days."

"If her father feels she requires medical treatment, he should take her to a proper doctor," her mother agreed.

"I think I'll suggest to Hazel she shouldn't take any more of those injections."

"It would be wise."

"She's taken them mostly to please her father," Carolyn worried, "but I think it's time she stopped catering to him."

"If it means injuring her health, that's surely true."

"Nicholas Freeze has a lot of crazy ideas," Carolyn complained.

Elizabeth's face showed gentle reproach. "I told you that before you made up your mind to spend your summer working for him but you wouldn't listen to me."

"I didn't understand how dangerous a person like him can be then," she offered in explanation.

"You don't have to stay on there. I'd be glad to have you leave."

"I won't as long as Hazel works for him. It wouldn't be fair to leave her after us planning the summer together."

"Why couldn't she take the summer off, also, and enjoy it here with you?" Elizabeth wanted to know.

Hope brightened Carolyn's face. "Perhaps she would consider doing that. I can ask her."

"I think you should. And warn her again about Dr. Blake."

Carolyn suggested, "Perhaps if you'd stop by and speak to her on your way to your room it might help."

"Very well. I'll stop and chat with her," Elizabeth promised.

Shortly afterward she went upstairs, and Carolyn was left alone in the living room. She was upset about Hazel's unhappy state and by the fact that for the second night there had been no sign of Barnabas. Then the front doorbell rang, and she hastened out to answer it.

Barnabas stood there in the drizzle in his caped coat "Am I welcome?" he asked.

"Very welcome," she exclaimed happily. "I'm all alone down here waiting for you."

He entered the hallway. "I saw the light and hoped I might find you."

She led him into the living room, and they stood under one of the great crystal chandeliers. She asked, "Why didn't you come here last night?"

There was an uneasiness in his deep-set eyes. "I had some urgent things to do."

"You went to the rehearsal?"

"Yes."

She studied him closely. "Of course you know another one of the girl hippies was attacked last night?"

"You've heard."

"Unfortunately. According to Uncle Roger, the police have been querying him about you and your habits."

His smile was bitter. "In that case I may soon have to move on."

"Surely there is some other way."

"I'll think about it," he said softly.

"There's something else." She gave him an account of the repeated liver injections Dr. Blake was giving Hazel.

"She probably doesn't need them," Barnabas said.

Carolyn gave him a meaningful look. "I thought she might, since you did rob her of some blood."

"Of only a tiny amount," he replied. "It wouldn't give her anemia. I think that condition is a figment of the doctor's imagination."

"I'm starting to think so," she agreed, "and I'm going to tell Hazel not to take any more of those injections."

"You most certainly should do that. Next thing they'll be wanting to give her that life potion."

"I'm afraid of that," she said unhappily.

"She should take a stand now."

"Maybe she will."

Barnabas was watching her with concerned eyes. "You don't sound too sure about it."

"I'm not," she confessed. "It's a difficult situation."

"Speaking of difficult situations," Barnabas said, "I'm finding Mike Buchanan a temperamental person to work under."

"Is he deliberately being hard on you?"

"Perhaps not," Barnabas said. "But there is a something about him that is antagonistic to me."

"He's jealous of your powers over Hazel. He's interested in her for himself."

"I gather that," Barnabas said, weighing his black cane in his hands.

"I'm sure Mike really is Quentin."

Barnabas smiled wryly. "Interesting, if true."

"Don't you agree?"

"I'm not all that sure yet," Barnabas said. "I should know by the time we've worked together a little longer. There are certain traits of Quentin's that are bound to betray him sooner or later."

"I've asked Jim Swift to help us by also keeping an eye on him," she said.

Barnabas's brown eyes twinkled. "You've come to like that young man, haven't you?"

"And to trust him."

"Don't ever forget he is an actor."

"What does that mean?"

"Theatre people are often extremely clever at concealing their true feelings," Barnabas warned her.

"I'm positive Jim is being frank with me," she said. "He's that type of person."

Barnabas laughed lightly. "Now I'm the one beginning to feel jealous."

She came close to him and said in a soft voice, "You needn't ever! But you refuse to take me seriously. Instead, you treat me like a child."

He took her by the arms. "A lovely child!"

Her eyes were troubled. "What is going to happen to all of us, Barnabas?"

"Nothing too disastrous, I trust."

"I can't think that way," she said. "I have a premonition that we're most of us headed for tragedy."

"You're allowing yourself to become a neurotic," he chided her.

She shook her head. "I somehow feel it. It's not going to be a happy summer."

"Don't dwell on such thoughts," Barnabas said and drew her close and this time kissed her on the lips. She felt the icy chill of his lips on hers and remembered that room in the cellar where he had rested in deathlike stillness in his casket. It almost made her draw back in revulsion but she somehow controlled herself with the thought that icy though the lips were, they belonged to a man she loved.

He released her and, his eyes still fixed on hers, said, "I must leave now. I have to get to the village for rehearsal."

Gazing up at him, she begged, "If you need someone's throat tonight, let it be mine. I won't mind."

"I'll think about it," he said gently as he started for the front door.

She saw him out into the drizzle and fog. His gallant figure was lost to her more quickly than usual because of the mist. With a sigh she closed the door and went upstairs.

Hazel was asleep so she undressed as quietly as she could and got into bed. As soon as she'd put out the last of the lights, she also fell asleep. When she awoke some time later, it was still dark. She consulted the luminous hands of her bedside clock and saw that it was nearly two in the morning.

She could hear the chant of a distant foghorn mixed with the wash of the waves on the rocky shore. She sat up and listened for some sound from Hazel's room, but it was all silence. In fact, the silence was frightening in itself. There was too much quiet. Her heart began to beat a trifle faster, and with fear tightening her throat she decided to get up from her bed and see if Hazel was all right.

Remembrance of the girl's pale face and her complaints of a headache mingled to make Carolyn concerned about her friend. What if the treatments had proved too strong and Hazel was seriously ill or even dead?

She moved quickly across the dark room to the doorway and peered toward her friend's bed. Still there was no sound of any stirring, or even of breathing. Panic mounted in Carolyn, and she advanced hesitantly into Hazel's bedroom. In a moment she was beside the bed – and then she knew the reason for the silence. The bed was empty!

Finding the wall switch she turned on the lights and saw that the bed had been slept in, but Hazel was not there now. At once the thought flashed through her mind that she had gone out into the night for another rendezvous with Barnabas.

Barnabas still had his spell cast over her so that she had left her bed to meet him again on the grounds. He would drink her blood, even though he'd made a promise that he wouldn't. The realization hurt Carolyn. In his desperation Barnabas had broken his word to her. He insisted these incidents did Hazel no harm, but Carolyn was by no means satisfied this was true.

Filled with turmoil, she went back to her own room and hastily put on a long maxi-raincoat and sports shoes. Extracting a flashlight from her bedside drawer, she left her room and went down the broad stairway to the ground floor of the house.

In the drizzle and heavy fog it would be hard to see anyone at a distance. To find Hazel and Barnabas she would be forced to search the garden. Bracing herself against the cold wetness of the Maine summer night, she went down the front steps. She started across the lawn, the wet grass soaking her shoes. She pulled the raincoat around her tightly and shone the flashlight through the murky fog.

Reaching the garden area she moved slowly, and then she

caught sight of a ghostly figure floating to her through the mist She fought back an impulse to cry out and shone her flashlight on the figure. It was Hazel coming toward her in her sleepwalking state, the flowing white nightgown giving her the air of a phantom, her long black hair curling around her shoulders.

Hazel was close to her now. The dark girl's eyes were wide and staring, yet she seemed to not see her at all. Like a spirit she glided past her and back in the direction of the mansion. It was clear to Carolyn that her friend was still under the hypnotic influence of Barnabas.

Anger at the man she loved seethed up in her. How could Barnabas do such a cruel thing and betray her in this way? She felt that Hazel would find her way into the house and back to her bed. It would be better not to awaken her suddenly and perhaps cause some dreadful reaction. Instead, she turned her energies to seeking out Barnabas. She wanted to release her pent-up anger by condemning him to his face for what he'd done.

She moved farther away from the house so that the sound of the foghorn and the roar of the waves were louder in her ears now. Her feet were soaked, and so was her hair, but she wasn't going to give up without trying to locate the man who'd broken his word to her.

She stood with the flashlight in hand, its beam creating a fuzzy yellow path through the fog but revealing nothing, and in a timorous voice called out, "Barnabas!"

There was no reply, so she moved on. The events of the recent few minutes had filled her with bitterness and hurt. She was wandering far from the house with no thought for her personal safety. She could only picture Barnabas somewhere there, standing forlornly in the fog, ashamed of what he'd done and hiding from her.

She halted and called out again, "Barnabas!"

This time the beam of her flashlight caught a motion from an area of bushes near her. She went forward a step as a figure began to emerge from the bushes. Suddenly she gave way to a scream, for the man who was striding to her from that place of hiding was not Barnabas, but the weird phantom she'd seen once before in the theatre – the man with a werewolf's ugly face!

CHAPTER 8

The strangely distorted features of the monster were made more so by the fog. Carolyn screamed out again and turned and fled. In her panic she let the flashlight drop, and so she hurtled across the wet lawn in complete darkness. Sobbing, she made her way toward the entrance door, not daring to hesitate or look back. At last she reached the steps and stumbled up them and threw the door open. Seconds later she was inside with the door closed between her and that demon of the night.

Breathless she sagged against the door. Her hair was dripping wet and her shoes a soggy mess. The raincoat had sheltered her nightgown and body, but the cold had reached her. So now she was shivering with fear and exposure. She'd seen no sign of Hazel, so she must have gotten to her room in safety.

Carolyn straightened and was about to cross the shadowed hallway to the stairs when she saw her Uncle Roger, clad in pajamas and dressing gown, advancing down to meet her.

"What does this mean?" he demanded sternly.

She stood there frozen with fright. It would be disastrous to tell the truth and reveal that Barnabas had been preying on their guest for her blood. Roger would find this the last straw and be ruthless in his treatment of the unfortunate Barnabas. She had to think up some excuse for her being down there in her pitiable condition.

Roger reached the bottom of the stairs and now advanced to face her. "You haven't answered me," he said.

She touched a hand to her temple. "I'm sorry. I'm still confused!"

"What were you doing out in the wet at this hour?"

Swallowing hard, she said, "I woke up and went to my window. I saw a strange figure on the lawn. It bothered me, and I went down to see who it was."

Roger's face indicated his disbelief. "Why didn't you call me?"

"I didn't want to bother you," she improvised. "I was afraid it might only be my imagination."

"So you came down alone and went outside with no protection?"

"I had my flashlight."

He shook his head grimly. "I wouldn't call that much to depend on. You know the things that have happened here lately, how dangerous the village has become at night. What made you do such a foolhardy thing?"

"It's hard to explain," she faltered.

"I can imagine," he said with disgust. "Go on."

"When I went out on the lawn, I saw nothing at first."

"So you ventured out farther, I suppose?"

"Yes."

"It's what I'd expect," he said grimly.

"I reached some bushes before I saw anything, and then it was just a blurred figure. I shone my flashlight in that direction, and it came out of the bushes. It was a man with an animal's features. It was so horrible I panicked and started running back to the house. Along the way I lost my flashlight."

Roger looked alarmed. "You saw a man with a face like an animal?"

"Yes. I don't know whether I was followed or not. I didn't dare look back. I'd just managed to get inside and close the door when you came down."

"You've told a remarkable story," he uncle said sternly.

"I know that."

"If what you say is true, we do indeed have new problems at Collinwood. It has to mean that Quentin has returned."

Her eyes widened. "Of course!" she said tensely. "The werewolf's head!"

"You're sure you saw this monstrous figure clearly?"

"I did when it came close, for just a fleeting second."

"It has to be Quentin," he said slowly.

"What can we do?"

"Nothing at this time of night except pray that he'll recover from his seizure and return to his normal self. He's only a menace when he's in the grip of the curse."

She had at least told him part of the truth. She had no doubt that the frightening apparition that had come after her from the bushes had been Quentin. She'd suspected he was in the village, and this seemed to prove it beyond question.

"I was an awful fool to go out there alone," she admitted.

Her uncle snorted. "I can only say you're right. You deserved whatever happened to you."

"I won't do such a thing again."

"You always say that, but you don't seem to learn," Roger snapped. "It's a wonder you haven't roused the whole house."

"I hope no one else hears us," she said, in a quieter voice.

"So do I," he agreed, lowering his own voice. Quickly he went to the window next to the front door and pulled aside the drape to glance out into the fog. He suddenly went rigid and then turned to her and in a tense voice said, "There's someone walking out there now."

Panic flooded her again. It would have to be Barnabas, and Roger would be enraged and begin to suspect there was more to the story than she'd revealed. She stood a distance away from him and said, "Are you sure?"

"Of course I am," Roger said, annoyed, as he threw the front door open to go out onto the steps. "You there!" he called.

Carolyn advanced to the door and saw the man coming through the fog toward them in answer to Roger's shout. Her heart began to pound. Then as he came near she felt relief. It was the director, Mike Buchanan.

Roger was in a rage. "What are you doing prowling around here?"

Mike took it calmly. He was wearing a trenchcoat and still had on his dark glasses. "I'm not prowling. I'm taking a stroll before going to bed."

"At this hour, it is prowling!" Roger snapped.

"Sorry," Mike said politely and glanced at her. "Hello, Carolyn. Are you a night person, too?"

Roger spoke up before she could answer, "Did you deliberately scare this girl?"

"Why do you ask that?" Mike said.

Roger glared at him from the top step. "Someone did, and you're the most likely suspect!"

She managed, "I don't think it could have been Mike."

"Thank you," Mike smiled coolly.

Her uncle took a deep breath. "Your rental of the cottage does not include the privilege to trespass on our lawns at night. I consider your being here an invasion of our privacy."

"It won't happen again," Mike assured him. "I had a late rehearsal and wanted to relax before I went to bed. I didn't pay any attention to where I was walking. At this time of night I thought it wouldn't matter."

"I say it matters a great deal," Roger Collins stormed. "You caused my niece to venture out into the wet night and then frightened her. If anything of this sort happens again, I'll be forced to ask you to vacate the cottage."

"I'll be careful in the future," Mike said, with that surprising patience.

But then it wasn't so surprising, Carolyn decided. Wasn't he Quentin? Wouldn't he try to conceal this from her uncle at all costs? Roger would now believe she'd been frightened by a shadow and her own imagination. He'd give up his belief that Quentin had returned, which was exactly what the calm young man standing there posing as Mike wanted.

"I'm completely serious about all this," Roger said in final warning.

"I've never doubted that," Mike assured him. "Goodnight to you both. I know you must want to return to bed." With a nod he turned and walked off.

Roger came in and closed the door. He frowned at her. "So now you know who your phantom was?"

"Mike doesn't have a wolf's face," she reminded him.

"In your fear you thought he had," was her uncle's comment.

"Perhaps," she said reluctantly, knowing it wasn't so, not wanting to cross her uncle if he was so set on believing it.

"You'd better go on up to bed before you see some other monsters," Roger said with disgust. "I wasn't bluffing when I told that young man that another error on his part and I'll no longer put up with him on the estate."

"He admitted he was wrong and agreed to abide by your decision," she reminded him.

"The thought of the upset he's caused still makes me angry," Roger said.

As they started up the stairway together, she gave him a searching glance and said, "You've decided that it couldn't have been Quentin?"

"Of course."

"What made you change your mind so quickly?"

"Finding Buchanan out there. He's the obvious answer to your nightmarish experience."

She sighed. "I hope you're right."

At the head of the stairs they halted before going different directions to their rooms. Roger regarded her sternly again. "Never, never do anything like this in the future."

"I know."

"My lectures seem to be always lost on you," he sighed, "but I'm deadly serious about this."

"I understand, and I've learned my lesson," she said.

"I hope so," he said without conviction. "Goodnight – what's left of it!"

They parted, and she went on to her own bedroom. She let herself in quietly and tiptoed to the doorway of Hazel's room to be sure her friend was safely in bed and asleep. She was! Satisfied, Carolyn went to her own bed. She found a towel and dried her hair and wet feet, then slipped between the sheets still shivering with nerves and cold.

Alone in the darkness there was no longer any need for the pretence she'd had to indulge in when her uncle was questioning her. Now her thoughts could be starkly clear. One thing was certain. She had a difference to settle with Barnabas. He had gone back on his word and preyed on the ailing Hazel again tonight.

And the sudden appearance of Mike Buchanan so soon after she'd seen the werewolf left no remaining doubt in her mind that he was Quentin. She had been coming to this belief for some time. Now she was sure, but what she was going to do about it was another matter. For the moment, she'd try to get warm and sleep. The morning would be time enough for decisions.

She dropped off to sleep clinging to this belief, little realizing the horror another day would bring.

The moment she awoke, before she dressed, she knew something was terribly wrong with Hazel. The moans and babblings of the girl in the other room came to her with terrifying clarity. She quickly got out of bed and hurried to the bedside of her friend.

Hazel stared up at her with wild, glazed eyes. "Choking!" was the only word she could make of her tortured babbling. Carolyn was sickened to see that she had evidently been tearing at her throat in the night. It was a mass of scratches and red irritated marks. She tossed from side to side and never ceased her tortured murmuring.

"I'll get Mother," Carolyn told her and ran back to her own room to put on her dressing gown.

Fortunately she met her mother in the corridor on her way down for breakfast. Breathlessly, she told her, "Hazel's awfully ill! Come quickly!"

Elizabeth followed her to the girl's room and tried to discover what seemed wrong with her. Hazel continued to murmur wildly and toss in the bed. It was impossible to communicate with her, and

Carolyn felt her condition had deteriorated in the short time since she'd first gone to her.

Elizabeth gave Carolyn a stricken glance. "I don't know what's wrong, but she is desperately ill."

"What can we do?" Carolyn asked.

"I'll go down and speak to your Uncle Roger," she said.

Feeling there was nothing she could do to help her stricken friend, Carolyn followed her mother down to the dining room. All the while she was suffering from pangs of conscience. Had this illness anything to do with the girl's rendezvous with Barnabas last night? If so, should she reveal what she knew? But that would be betraying Barnabas, and she didn't want to do that until she was certain he was in the wrong.

When they entered the dining room, Roger looked up from his plate with annoyance. "What now?"

"Hazel Freeze is dreadfully ill," Elizabeth announced.

Roger threw down his fork. "Another crisis," he said angrily. "I felt taking that girl in here was a bad error."

"Don't go on about that. What are we going to do?" Elizabeth demanded.

Roger rose from the table. "I'll call her father."

"Shouldn't we get a doctor?" Carolyn wanted to know.

Her uncle shot her an angry glance. "Freeze can have a doctor here as soon as we can. And he should make the decision. He should also decide who it is going to be."

"He'll send that awful old Dr. Blake," Carolyn predicted with dismay.

"It's his choice," Roger pointed out coldly as he left them to make the phone call.

Carolyn turned to her mother in panic. "I think we should call our own doctor."

Elizabeth looked upset. "Roger is right. If Hazel is as ill as she seems, we have no right to accept all the responsibility. If anything happened, her father could blame us."

"If anything happened!" Carolyn repeated in despair. "You can't think she's going to die?"

Her mother was clearly distressed. "I didn't say that. But you must have seen she's a very sick girl."

"Probably Dr. Blake made her sick with all those liver injections," she said angrily.

"We just don't know yet," her mother placated her.

"Her father is a hateful person, mean and nasty," Carolyn said, "and he's a friend of that awful drunken Dr. Blake, so he'll be sure to send him to treat Hazel and he won't do her any good."

"Wait until Roger brings us some word," her mother advised

her.

"I can't bear it!" Carolyn wailed, tears brimming in her eyes. She was thinking about Barnabas and that it wouldn't be until nightfall that she'd be able to hear his side of what happened. Could she depend on herself to keep her lips closed about last night's incident until then?

Roger came striding back with his lips firmly pressed. He gave them a grim glance. "Freeze and the doctor are coming here at once."

"At least Mr. Freeze is coming," Elizabeth said. "Is he bringing Dr. Blake?"

"I gathered that from the phone conversation," Roger said with a sigh. "But the old man didn't really make it clear. He seemed more concerned about the expense of having the doctor come here than anything else."

Carolyn said, "I'd better go up and stay with her until they arrive."

"Yes," Elizabeth agreed. "I'll join you in a few minutes."

As Carolyn started on her way, Roger called after her, "Be careful! Don't try to doctor her in any way. You could do her harm!"

She made no attempt to reply, but hurried on up the stairs. Her uncle's caution in the face of a crisis always came as a surprise to her but this morning it seemed more incongruous than ever. She'd barely noticed what sort of day it was. As she rushed down the hall, she glanced out one of the windows and saw that it was still foggy and drizzling. Sometimes these spells lasted several days.

Entering Hazel's room she was shocked to find the girl had moved on to another stage in her illness. Now she lay there motionless and staring up at the ceiling with eyes that seemed to see nothing. When Carolyn spoke to her, there was no response. She was barely breathing. Carolyn touched a hand to her friend's head and was shocked by how hot it was. She raced to the bathroom and wetted some washcloths in cold water and brought them back to apply to Hazel's forehead and temples.

She was sitting by the side of the bed doing this when she heard the arrival of Hazel's father and the doctor. The reedy voice of Nicholas Freeze and the rasping tones of the alcoholic Dr. Blake mixed with the stern statements of Roger as they came up the stairway. Carolyn rose and braced herself for the moments ahead.

Dr. Eric Blake, bag in hand and a furtive expression on his bloated, red face, led the way into the sickroom. He showed mild surprise on seeing her and then went on to examine the patient.

Nicholas Freeze entered with Roger and Elizabeth trailing behind him. When he saw her, the old man's wrinkled face took on a sly look. "I've said from the start Hazel isn't a well girl and she's been working too hard. That's why I insisted she have those liver injections."

Carolyn couldn't resist telling him, "I believe those injections were what made her ill."

Nicholas Freeze shook his head irritably. "Couldn't be!"

"Why not?"

"The Doc said they were perfectly safe," he wheezed.

Roger spoke up. "The main thing is to find her trouble now. I don't think we should all be in here crowding the patient and doctor. We should wait in the hall."

They moved into the hall, an uneasy little group as they waited in morose silence for some announcement from Dr. Blake. It was quite a few minutes before he came out rather unsteadily.

Very professionally, he said, "The young woman is the victim of some kind of virus. She needs a series of antibiotics and the care of a professional nurse. I'm going to take her to my place and have my nurse look after her."

Nicholas rushed over to the doctor. "Can you save her, Doctor?"

"I think so," Dr. Blake said. "But it's essential to move her at once."

"Is she well enough to be moved?" Elizabeth worried. "Shouldn't she go to a hospital?"

Roger demanded. "I think she should be taken directly to the Ellsworth Hospital. She'll get the best care there."

"No need for her to be in a hospital," Dr. Blake said stubbornly. "As a medical man I'd say it was too long a trip for her in her present state."

Carolyn was frantic. "Are you sure you're properly equipped to give her every care at your place?"

"Yes," Dr. Blake said, scowling at her. "If someone will help, we can wrap the young woman in a few blankets and carry her to my car."

So Carolyn was forced to sit by and watch while her friend was practically being abducted. "How ill is she?" she asked for need of better words, but her mind was in a reeling turmoil.

Dr. Eric Blake said soberly, "She has no more than an even chance to recover."

Events continued at the same hectic pace. In spite of Carolyn's mild protests, the sick girl was wrapped in blankets and carried down to the back seat of the doctor's big black limousine. Before they drove away, Nicholas Freeze turned to her and muttered something about it being all right for her to take the day off.

As the car drove away leaving Roger, Elizabeth, and Carolyn standing at the bottom of the front steps watching it, Roger Collins said, "I suppose it sounds cruel on my part, but I'm glad to see that girl out of the house!"

Carolyn's mother gave him a startled glance. "You are cruel, Roger. That poor child is dreadfully ill."

"And of some unknown disease," Roger grumbled. "I'm glad to see her in her father's care. I wouldn't be surprised if she died!"

"Neither would I, considering her doctor," Carolyn said unhappily. "I think we all played into the hands of Nicholas Freeze. He wants to get full control of Hazel."

Roger eyed her stonily. "We can't afford to be sentimental in a crisis. It is his right to have charge of her."

"It's all wrong!" Carolyn wailed as she ran into the house.

She went to her own room for a good cry. She couldn't bear to go into the room Hazel had occupied. The sight of her friend's belongings and the hints of her presence there would be too much to bear.

After a while her mother came to her and sat on the bed beside her outstretched form. Patting her gently on the shoulder, she said, "You mustn't give way to despair this way. You may be surprised. Hazel may get better quickly, once the doctor starts his treatments."

She sighed deeply. "I feel she's doomed!"

"That's being childish," Elizabeth said. "Mr. Freeze said you could have the day off. I think you should go into the village and keep in touch with Hazel's progress. You'll meet some other people and talk to them. It will help you get through this crisis."

She sat up. "I don't feel like talking to anyone."

"You will," her mother said. "I hear you had a nasty experience last night. Roger told me just now about that director fellow scaring you."

"It's not important!"

"I think it was," she argued. "You lost your rest and so aren't as well prepared for today as you should be. That young man was thoughtless to behave as he did."

Carolyn got to her feet "I'm not sure Roger has all the facts right."

"He seems to think he has."

"That's one of his faults," Carolyn said unhappily. Then, as she realized what a day staying at Collinwood might be like, she added, "I guess I will drive to the village, after all."

Her mother gave her a weary smile. "I told you it would be the best thing to do."

On her way out to the car Carolyn met Roger, who was leaving for the factory. He halted the car and, sticking his head out the window, told her, "You should send Hazel some flowers when you're in the village."

"She'd be better off with a good doctor," she told him, still resentful that he'd not sent for their family doctor.

Her uncle's face resumed its stern lines. "I did what was best," he snapped as he drove on.

She got into the station wagon, missing Hazel at her side. When she drove into the village she went directly to the "Olde Antique Barn." The only one there was Tom Buzzell. He was sitting in the office, behaving like the proprietor for once.

He greeted her with a worried look on his sunken face. "Nicholas is over to the Doc's place. He left me in charge. Guess Hazel is pretty bad off."

Standing in the middle of the dingy office, she asked, "Have they found out what her trouble is yet?"

"Nope. Not that I've heard," the handyman said. "But I've known for some while back that gal wasn't long for this world!"

Carolyn stared at him. "What makes you say that?"

"I can tell," he assured her solemnly. "Voices from the spirit world whisper things to me. Almost every time I passed her here in the barn, I'd hear that soft whisper, 'She's going to die!' "

It was ridiculous and almost obscene, with Hazel so ill, but this account of ghostly whisperings actually sent a ripple of cold terror through her. Was Tom Buzzell so mad from his excessive drinking that he'd really come to the point of hearing voices and believing in them?

"That's a dreadful thing to say!" Carolyn gasped.

"Them's the whispers I heard," Tom said solemnly. "I've heard them about others, and they died. So I know!"

"I don't want to hear any more such talk," she said, feeling ill. "I'm going to Doctor Blake's house."

"They won't let you in," Tom told her as she left. She paid no attention to him, and instead, got into the station wagon and drove to the side street where Doctor Blake's tumbledown old house was situated. In its day it had been a fine property but with his drinking he'd let it fall into ruin as he had everything else.

Parking in front of the door, she got out and went and rang the bell. The Doctor answered the door himself. She could smell the aroma of liquor on his breath and saw that his eyes were glazed.

"How is Hazel?" she demanded.

"I'm doin' what I can for her," he said, avoiding her eyes.

"What are you treating her for?"

"Virus. Unknown virus. Very difficult," he said, slurring his words.

Again she knew frustration and fear. "May I see her for a moment?"

He waved her off drunkenly. "No. Father forbids it. For her good. I'll let you know how she is later."

"I'd like to see her now," Carolyn protested. "Just to look at her from the doorway."

"Impossible," the drunken Dr. Blake said, and to reinforce his statement he went back inside and shut the door in her face.

She stood there, shocked, not knowing what to do. She couldn't appeal to anyone to challenge the drunken medico's authority. Hazel's father had put him in charge of the case, and that settled it!

After a moment she slowly went back to the car and headed it for the main street. It was her plan to drive to the plant and try to talk her Uncle Roger into taking more interest in Hazel's fate, at least to the point of sending word to her aunt.

But while she was turning into the main street she saw Jim Swift coming down the City Hall steps. He'd apparently been up in the theatre doing some work. He also spotted her and waved to her frantically to halt by the entrance to the building.

He came hurrying over to the car. "What's this I hear about Hazel being ill?" he asked, leaning down by the window.

She was startled. "How have you heard so soon?"

"I went to the barn to select some pieces for the show, and that Tom Buzzell told me," Jim said.

"Oh," she said, relaxing. "Come in and sit in the car for a moment and I'll tell you about it." He got in the car beside her and she gave him all the details, except for the fact that Hazel had been out to meet Barnabas, which she still was saving for the time when she saw Barnabas face to face.

Jim was frowning. "What do you think caused her sudden illness?"

"I'd say those liver injections. She didn't need them. And that drunken Dr. Blake surely gave her too many."

Jim shot her a meaningful look. "Are you sure it was liver injections he was giving her?"

The question hit her with shattering impact! Suddenly she realized she'd missed the most obvious explanation. All the talk of Nicholas Freeze and the doctor about giving the unfortunate Hazel liver injections had been a bluff. From the start they must have been injecting the elixir of life into her veins!

CHAPTER 9

"I'd never thought of that," Carolyn admitted.

Jim Swift seemed deadly serious. "It might pay you to. You never can tell what error a doctor like Blake might make."

Her eyes met his. "Or what he would do deliberately," she said in a taut voice.

"Have you any reason to suspect him of treating her with something else?" Jim wanted to know.

She was unwilling to discuss the potion with the young actor at this point. First she wanted to ask Hazel's father some questions and then talk to Barnabas about his role in all that had happened. It bothered her that Barnabas might still bear some guilt for Hazel's being suddenly stricken.

Staring through the windshield at the busy traffic she said, "I'm very confused. I must think about this. But I'm glad you brought up the possibility."

Jim was sympathetic. "You and Hazel are close friends. This is hard on you."

"Especially as I feel some responsibility for her illness."

"Why should you?"

She didn't answer at once. For the time being, she must act warily to protect Barnabas, and she still wasn't sure that Hazel's father and Blake had given her friend the dangerous youth potion. She had to find out more of what had gone on.

Finally, she said, "Hazel was my guest. She became ill at Collinwood."

"You shouldn't let that bother you. It could have happened anywhere," he said.

"I suppose so."

"She may recover soon in spite of Dr. Blake. Don't worry too much," Jim comforted her.

"I do wish she was in other hands," she said with a sigh. "But her father and Dr. Blake are cronies."

"Not much you can do then," he said dryly.

"No. How did your rehearsal go last night?"

"Fine. Barnabas is a good actor."

"I couldn't sleep, and I went out for a walk after midnight," she told him. "I was strolling in the fog and I had a dreadful experience."

"What sort of experience?" Jim looked interested.

"I saw that monstrous figure that frightened me in the auditorium the night of our first meeting."

"Again?"

"Yes. I was beginning to believe I'd made a mistake that first time, that perhaps it had been the shadows in the empty auditorium which cast a pattern on some normal face and made it seem grotesque. But last night I saw the identical animal features – a man with a werewolf's distorted visage!"

Jim frowned. "Did the thing harm you, or attempt to?"

"I ran back to the house. As far as I know, I wasn't followed."

"This monster you've described vanished?"

"Yes."

"Have you any explanation for it?"

She hesitated, knowing that Jim Swift was her friend but worrying about how understanding he might be in this matter. Then, on impulse, she decided to confide in him.

She said, "I believe the werewolf may be a relative of mine, Quentin Collins."

Jim Swift raised his eyebrows. "The one I've heard Mike Buchanan talking about? I thought he'd left here long ago."

Carolyn's eyes met his solemnly. "He did, but I believe he has returned. In fact, I suspect that Mike Buchanan is Quentin."

It was Jim's turn to show utter surprise. "That's pretty fantastic, isn't it?"

"Not as much so as it may seem," she advised him.

"Mike is the last one I'd think of as Quentin," he said.

"How much do you really know about him?"

"Not all that much," the actor admitted.

"I'll bet it's the same with the others," she told him. "From the start, Mike seems to have known too much about the history of Collinwood and Quentin. I wondered how he became so familiar with all the details. Now I think I know."

Jim frowned as he considered this. "Mike was back at the cottage around midnight. He always goes out for a stroll after he gets home."

"I know," she said. "After I saw the monster, my uncle and I spotted Mike walking near the entrance to Collinwood."

"So he was nearby when it all happened?"

"Yes, and he had no proper explanation for being there."

"That needn't mean he was the monster," Jim argued. "He could have innocently walked into the situation."

"I wonder."

Jim sat back against the seat. "I don't blame you for having doubts about him. So would I in your place."

"You weren't with him at the cottage last night?"

"No. He drove home in his own car. I drove mine to my boarding house and went to bed early."

"If Mike is really Quentin, we are in for some trouble," she said.

"Is he such a wicked character?"

"I don't believe so," she admitted. "But he is subject to spells when he isn't fully responsible. At those times there is reason for apprehension. And Barnabas being here as well doubles the problems."

"He is rather eccentric," the actor agreed.

"People in the village are suspicious of them both," Carolyn worried. "I don't know whether rightly or wrongly. I only wish things hadn't gotten so complicated."

"Is there anything I can do?"

"No more than I asked before," she said. "Keeping a close watch on Mike for anything to indicate he could be Quentin would be helpful."

"I'll continue doing that," he promised. "I only wish we had more free time for each other. The way it has been, neither of us seems to have many idle minutes."

She smiled wistfully. "In spite of that, we've become good friends."

"I'd like to see us get to know each other better."

"The tension may ease and allow us time together later."

"I hope so," he sighed. "I think Barnabas is getting all the breaks in that respect. No wonder he's charmed you."

"We've been friends for ages."

Jim looked unhappy. "I don't think you really take any notice of other men. So what chance have I got with you?"

She eyed him gently. "I take enough notice of you to realize I like you very much. And you know it."

"I hope that's true," he said. "I'll cross my fingers that Hazel recovers quickly."

"That's the main worry now," Carolyn agreed. "Once she's well, everyone will be less tense."

Jim left her shortly and went strolling down the main street, while she drove back to Collinwood to give a report of events to her mother. All the way back in the car she went over the facts of Hazel's illness in her mind. She could see only two possible reasons for its sudden impact; either she had suffered through the meetings with Barnabas and the drain on her blood, or Nicholas Freeze and Dr. Blake had tricked the unfortunate girl into taking the ancient potion while making her believe the injections contained liver extract.

Jim Swift's suggestion had more meaning for her than he could possibly have realized. If Hazel had received the dangerous injections without suspecting it, she had also been completely deceived. The more she thought about it, the more likely it seemed to her that Nicholas Freeze had deliberately condemned his daughter to the experiment.

Reaching Collinwood she searched out her mother in the sunporch. Elizabeth was crocheting and stopped in the midst of it to listen to her daughter's report on Hazel's condition and her suspicions about the youth potion.

Elizabeth listened with her brow furrowed. "You didn't tell me anything about finding those three ancient bottles and the faded document with them?"

"I knew Nicholas Freeze didn't want me to talk about it."

"I can't believe this so-called elixir can truly possess any quality to add to longevity," her mother worried, "or to retain youth. And if Nicholas Freeze thinks so, he must be slightly mad."

"I'm sure that he is," Carolyn agreed.

Elizabeth considered the matter with a shadowed expression on her lovely face. "I wouldn't mention this to your Uncle Roger, he becomes upset so easily. There's no telling how he'd react."

"I had to talk it over with someone," she said.

"I'm glad you told me," her mother said. "But I don't see any action you can take. Hazel may get well and the entire problem will be solved. At this stage of things you can't accuse Nicholas Freeze of poisoning his daughter through those injections of Dr. Blake's."

"I know that."

"Even if Hazel should die, I don't believe you could make the accusation stick unless the authorities found some poison in her body. They'd consider your story fantastic, especially if Dr. Blake and

Nicholas Freeze denied the alchemist's elixir ever existed."

"But it does exist and there was a warning about its use," Carolyn said unhappily, "and Barnabas knows there was a John Wykcliffe."

"It is possible Barnabas may have some ideas," her mother said. "At the moment it seems to me we can only wait and hope for Hazel's recovery."

Carolyn was forced to realize the wisdom of this advice, and so the day continued, one of painful waiting.

When evening came, she walked over to the old house ready for her confrontation with Barnabas. Never before had she felt herself lined up against him. Now she wasn't sure. If he had harmed Hazel, he could no longer be her friend.

Dusk was flooding the evening as she reached the door of the shuttered old brick house. Barnabas should have roused himself from his casket in that drab cellar room. She mounted the steps and rapped on the door and waited. After a moment there was the sound of approaching footsteps inside, and Barnabas came and opened the door for her.

His handsome, somewhat sallow face showed a welcoming smile. "What a pleasant surprise," he said. "Come in."

"I had to talk to you alone," she told him in a restrained voice as she entered the dark hallway.

He closed the door after her and took her by the arm as they walked down the hall to the double doors of the living room. "You sound upset."

"I am," she admitted.

Barnabas led her to a chair by the fireplace and then stood facing her with his back to its ashes. "Tell me what is bothering you," he said.

Her eyes reproved him. "You broke your word to me last night!"

"Why do you say that?" he asked, with apparent surprise.

"Hazel left her bed and wandered around outside."

"I wasn't responsible!"

"I hope you're being honest with me, Barnabas," Carolyn said, her face pale.

"Haven't I always been?"

"Up until now."

"Why should you doubt me now?"

Her expression remained troubled. "Because I know you exerted a spell over Hazel for several nights and took blood from her."

"I admitted to that and the desperation that led me into doing it." Barnabas sounded upset.

"And I asked that you never do it again."

"I pledged that I wouldn't. I have kept my word."

Their eyes met, hers searching and unsatisfied. "I must have the absolute truth, Barnabas. I woke up last night, and Hazel had left her bed. She wandered outside in a sleepwalking state the same as that night when she had a rendezvous with you."

He spread his hands. "She had no rendezvous with me last night. If she suffered a sleepwalking interlude, and it is not all that uncommon, I had nothing to do with it."

"You swear?"

"Yes," Barnabas said. "You should know I wouldn't deliberately lie to you."

Carolyn was on her feet "I want to believe that, but something dreadful has happened. I was afraid you might be responsible."

"Explain," Barnabas urged her.

She quickly gave him the details of Hazel's illness, ending with, "If you had no part in what happened, I'll have to assume that Dr. Blake, acting under her father's orders, gave her that dangerous elixir."

Barnabas nodded. "It's undoubtedly what's happened. Nicholas is eager to try and reap a financial harvest on his discovery. He's used Hazel as a test case."

"What can we do?" Carolyn asked frantically.

"I'll try to scare the truth out of Blake," Barnabas said.

"How?"

His face was set. "I have my ways."

"To complicate matters, I saw the werewolf again last night on the lawn at Collinwood when I'd gone out to search for Hazel. But I didn't see the monster until after she'd returned to the house. Then it emerged from the bushes."

"Quentin again!"

"I'm afraid so," she said. She went on to add how Roger had come downstairs and they'd both discovered Mike Buchanan walking alone out there. "So there no longer can be any doubt Mike is Quentin in disguise."

"I'm inclined to agree," Barnabas said. "I've been studying him at the theatre, and he reminds me of Quentin in many ways."

She looked at him worriedly. "Is he your natural enemy? Will he try to hurt you?"

"I don't think so," he said, "though there is a certain weakness in him that could lead him into trouble."

"As if we haven't enough of that," she said despairingly.

"I don't think you should give too much thought to Quentin," he advised. "We must concentrate on Hazel and her fate."

"I agree."

Barnabas sighed. "I want you to go back to Collinwood and wait for me there. I'm paying a visit to the village on my own. When I return, I'll meet you at Collinwood and tell you what I've found out."

"You shouldn't let Roger see you arrive. He'll be suspicious something is going on. He's so short-tempered now, Mother feels it is best he be kept in the dark about this until we have more information."

"Go up to the Captain's Walk on the rooftop around ten o'clock," Barnabas told her. "I'll meet you there."

She stared at him. "Is that the best spot?"

"It will make it easy for me," Barnabas said without explaining. He embraced her and gave her a gentle kiss with those cold lips after which he saw her to the door of Collinwood.

She chatted with her mother in the living room for a few minutes and then went up to her own room. When it came close to ten, she would go to the roof and the Captain's Walk to wait for the return of Barnabas. She was very anxious to have his report on Hazel's condition and learn if he obtained any information from the drunken Dr. Blake.

As it drew near ten, she became extremely nervous. She had a feeling that the sinister shadows were closing in on her again. A premonition of bad news haunted her. All the ghosts of Collinwood were posturing for her from the dark corners of the old house. With a growing apprehension she left her room and made her way up the dark stairs to the rooftop.

Barnabas wasn't there, which was a shock in itself. She stood by the railing staring out at the star-studded sky and the ocean below. Far to the left were the twinkling lights of Collinsport, where Hazel was waging her battle for life, and to the right were Widows Hill, Collinsport Point, and the lighthouse whose beam intermittently swept across the ocean and bay.

Carolyn rarely came to this rooftop spot, and never alone. Now she trembled slightly as she stood there in the quiet darkness. She allowed herself to gaze far down below and see the dim reflection of the front entrance light. It made her dizzy. Suddenly she was aware of the unexpected, terrifying sound of the flapping of heavy wings somewhere above her. She glanced up, but saw nothing. A moment later Barnabas stepped out from behind a chimney.

"I'm a few minutes late," he said in his low, pleasant voice.

"I don't mind as long as you're here," she said.

He stood before her in the shadows and then, taking her by the arms, said, "You must brace yourself for some unpleasant news."

She gazed into his stern face with terrified eyes. "What is it?"

His hands gripped her firmly. "Hazel is dead."

"No!" It escaped her in a wail.

"I warned you the news was bad," Barnabas said and held her close to him.

"She was murdered!" Carolyn said as she clung to him, sobbing, her face against his chest. "Her father and Dr. Blake murdered her!"

"I'm not sure they meant to do it," he tried to console her. "But they surely injected that elixir into her veins."

"They must be punished!"

"That is another matter," he said grimly. "I don't know what Dr. Blake will give as the cause of her death. I have a notion he will carefully alibi himself."

Tears were running down her cheeks as she stared into his handsome face again. "You must be able to do something!"

"We'll see," he said. "Hazel apparently died only a short time ago. I don't know when they'll let you have the word."

"Did you talk to Dr. Blake?"

"Briefly," he said. "I found out it was the elixir they were giving Hazel, but he insists it is a harmless concoction."

"He doesn't know!"

"When I left him, I went on to the antique barn," Barnabas said. "I was surprised to find that Nicholas Freeze had a visitor."

"Wasn't he shattered by the news of Hazel's death?"

"He seemed more upset than shattered, more nervous than sorrowful," Barnabas replied. "His visitor was Mike Buchanan. He has no part in this week's play, so he is able to leave the theatre while the show is on."

She was astounded. "What was he doing there with Nicholas Freeze? Tonight of all times?"

"I'm not sure," Barnabas said. "But I do know they weren't happy about my arriving and finding them together."

"What did Hazel's father say to you?"

"He went on about her death, but I had the impression he was pretending grief rather than actually feeling it."

"He's still thinking of how he'll cash in on that elixir. I'm sorry I ever found it!"

"It's not your fault that he tried to use it," Barnabas said. "I think he and Mike, or Quentin if you like to call him that, were cooking up some plan when I interrupted them."

"What do you think it might be?"

"That's hard to say. Mike wouldn't be involved in Hazel's death, though, he seemed to like her well enough."

"He did pay her a lot of attention."

Barnabas frowned. "I think they're working together on

some sort of scheme to peddle the elixir. I say that because I know of nothing else to join them in such a conspiratorial manner, and because Dr. Blake hinted the potion would be supplied to others and would prove a boon to mankind."

Carolyn gasped. "That's horrible! Do they intend to go on killing people the same way they killed Hazel?"

"Nicholas Freeze probably wouldn't care if it meant a profit for him," Barnabas said.

Carolyn brushed a hand across her forehead. "I'm stunned. I can't believe Hazel is dead."

"I predict you'll have a phone call from old Nicholas the first thing in the morning," Barnabas said.

It turned out that he was right. Roger took the call early in the morning, and when Carolyn and her mother joined him at breakfast, he gave them the sad word. It came as no surprise for Carolyn. Her night had been a bad one with little sleep.

She asked her uncle, "What did Nicholas Freeze say was the cause of Hazel's death?"

"Pernicious anemia combined with some unknown virus," Roger said. "I never thought the girl too healthy."

Elizabeth spoke up, "She seemed well enough to me until she took that last spell. Have the funeral arrangements been made?"

Roger nodded. "It will be a private funeral with a closed casket."

Carolyn gave him a stunned look. "Why?"

He shrugged. "I have no idea. I suppose it's some whim of her father's. You know what he's like."

Carolyn had her own ideas. She felt there were some other ulterior motives for this needless secrecy. Still, there was nothing they could do. The "Olde Antique Barn" was closed for several days because of Hazel's death.

The night after the funeral, Carolyn and Barnabas went to the small cemetery in the village after dusk. Hazel had been buried there in a lot owned by her father's family. The cemetery adjoined the church and had a white picket fence. She and Barnabas stood in the twilight staring down at the fresh earth of the new grave.

"I can't believe any of it yet," she said in a choked voice. "Especially that Hazel is here in this grave."

"Your feelings are easy to understand," Barnabas said quietly.

"I'll never go inside that antique barn again," Carolyn declared. "Her father can hire someone else."

Barnabas gave her a strange look. "I was going to talk to you about that."

"You were?" She looked at him warily.

"Yes. I think you should return to your job there."

"Why?"

There was a gentle stirring of the leaves in the cemetery's tall shade trees as Barnabas hesitated before answering. "Because I want you to spy on Nicholas Freeze in the same fashion you've asked Jim Swift to spy on Mike Buchanan."

Her eyes widened. "You think it is that important?"

"I do, or I wouldn't suggest it."

"What could you hope to gain?"

"I am of the opinion that Nicholas Freeze and Mike, or Quentin if you prefer, are formulating a plan to sell the elixir. It's possible you may be able to learn what they're up to if you remain there."

"Isn't it a matter for the police? I'm sure the undertaker and that drunken Dr. Blake faked Hazel's death certificate. If her body were exhumed, couldn't we pin the guilt where it belongs – on Mr. Freeze and his cronies?"

"Not yet," Barnabas said. "We need additional proof."

Carolyn sighed deeply. "You want me to take on my job again?"

"If he asks you, and I predict that he will," Barnabas said.

Once again a prediction of his turned out to have value. The next day Nicholas Freeze paid a personal call on Carolyn and her mother. The old man was extremely sad and humble.

"I want you to come back to work," he said. "I miss having someone young around. You could make me happy. I think it is what Hazel would have wanted."

Carolyn despised his hypocritical behavior and words, but she pretended to consider his offer. "I don't know," she said.

Her mother said, "It is entirely up to my daughter. I will not force her. I can understand it will be very depressing for her to work for you again with Hazel gone."

Nicholas Freeze's rheumy eyes fixed on her urgently. "I will give you a raise in salary if you'll change your mind and come back."

"Very well," she said. "I'll return for the balance of the summer."

Her Uncle Roger was annoyed when he heard her decision, but he wasn't able to change her mind. He agreed she should continue to have the use of the station wagon, but requested that she not work any nights so she'd avoid having to drive home after dark alone. Carolyn promised to try to make this arrangement, though she doubted if Mr. Freeze would stand by it.

She had only taken the position because Barnabas had suggested it. She was still shaken by Hazel's death and really in no fit shape to work, but if she could somehow prevent Nicholas Freeze and the spurious Mike Buchanan from making an effort to profit by the elixir she meant to.

Barnabas had cautioned her to be careful. "Don't allow them to guess you suspect them, or it could be dangerous for you."

"I realize that," she agreed.

"Stay as close to the old man as you can," he'd instructed her, "and try to overhear any conversations he has with Mike Buchanan."

This didn't turn out to be as easy as it seemed. Whenever Mike arrived, and he was paying many furtive visits to the old barn, he and Nicholas quickly went into the office and locked the door against her. It was a frustrating business, and Carolyn learned little.

She also had to put up with Tom Buzzell's bleak warnings. The alcoholic handyman said with conviction, "Hazel's spirit is still wandering about the barn. I've seen her, and I can hear her. She's worried about you."

"Please, Tom," she reproved him. She didn't believe his tall tales and felt them to be a desecration of her dead friend's memory.

But then came the first Friday night of her being on the job without Hazel. Nicholas Freeze came to her and tremulously inquired whether she'd work for an extra hour or two in the evening. She had little choice but to say that she would.

"I need some Bennington jugs," he said in his reedy voice. "Would you go up to the second floor and see if you can find any?"

She agreed and left him to take care of the task. She had ventured up into the second-level regions of the barn rarely since Hazel's death, and now she did so filled with misgivings. Once again, as she mounted the plank steps to the upper floor, she had that weird feeling of oppression – of an unknown danger close to her!

CHAPTER 10

The world of antiques had always seemed to her to be weirdly close to the world of the dead. The dust-covered and cobweb-ridden treasures that filled the shadowed antique barn had once been the prized belongings of those whose skulls grinned into the blackness of rotted coffins deep down under the earth. Or perhaps their owners' skeletons were stretched out in dusty caskets in tombs like those she'd visited in the Collins family cemetery. Wherever these phantoms of the past might be, it wasn't too fantastic to expect their bony hands to reach out and frantically try to regain their possessions.

Flashlight in hand, she slowly mounted the rough steps. She resented having to work at night. Uncle Roger would be angry, and she also might miss seeing Barnabas. This latter worried her more than anything else. She debated whether to go straight home after her chores at the barn or to go to the theatre. Barnabas was playing nightly in the Ibsen play, and when it was over he would drive home with her. She made up her mind this would be best.

She reached the second level and hesitated, trying to decide where she could locate the Bennington jugs. She had seen some up there, but couldn't exactly place the spot. The few single bulbs hanging at intervals from the peaked roof did not provide enough light to see anything clearly and she depended on her flashlight for close-range inspection.

Her memory told her the jugs were at a counter about midway down the barn opposite the place where Nicholas Freeze kept his most precious items locked up. She made her way along the creaky board floor. The place had never seemed so macabre and frightening when Hazel was alive and there with her. Now its grim shadows suggested phantoms at every turn. Carolyn was anxious to get her errand done and go back downstairs. At least down there she'd have some company, and the feeling of ghostly presences wouldn't be so terrifying.

She reached the counter and inspected its wares with her flashlight There were jugs of every type and size on display, but so mixed up she had trouble sorting through them. They were also grimy with dust. Since Hazel's death, very little had been done. As she frowned over her task, she suddenly heard a scraping noise from behind her.

It set her nerves on edge, and a cold finger of fear touched her spine. When she slowly turned to see what the sound meant, her eyes fixed on the door of the locked room. She was stunned to see that it was slowly opening. Just a little at a time, but continuing to open gradually. Then the darkness revealed the sight of a phantom she'd never expected to see. The pale, ghostly form of Hazel in her flowing nightgown!

The ghost looked at her in fear and pain and uttered a low moaning sound! Carolyn screamed and turned to grope her way along the narrow alley between the counters that led to the stairway. She stumbled and sobbed and then resumed her flight, the flashlight still in her hand. Somehow she got down to the bottom of the rough stairway to race toward the office and the open barn door.

Before she reached the office, Mike Buchanan came to stand in her way. "What's the rush?"

Gasping as she stared at him wildly in the semi-darkness, she said, "I've seen a ghost!"

"A ghost?" His tone was incredulous.

She pointed back to the steps weakly. "Up there."

He studied her with open derision. "You're making a fool of yourself with your nerves."

His reproach coming on top of her shock was a staggering blow, at least until she realized that she was talking to Quentin, not Mike, and that he was opposed to her making any discoveries about what had gone on in the old barn.

"I saw Hazel's ghost. She moaned to me!" Carolyn insisted.

"You know better than that," Mike Buchanan said impatiently.

Nicholas Freeze appeared from the shadows to stand beside Mike. "What's wrong?" he asked in a quavering voice.

Mike turned to him with a sneer. "She claims she's just seen your daughter's ghost."

"Hazel's ghost!" Nicholas echoed.

"I did," she said, feeling as if she might faint.

"What kind of monstrous lie are you telling?" Mr. Freeze demanded loudly.

"I saw Hazel. She was coming out of your private room. The door opened a little at a time."

The wrinkled face showed both anger and terror. He came quickly to her and wrested the flashlight from her weak grasp. "I'll soon find out whether we have a ghost there or not!" he exclaimed, and he went hobbling quickly by her to ascend the plank steps in his crab-like fashion.

Left alone with her, Mike said, "You shouldn't have come down here with a story like that. How do you think he feels?"

"I did see a ghost."

"You heard a sound and saw a shadow, and your imagination did the rest," he assured her. "Hazel is six feet under ground in the cemetery."

"I don't care," she argued.

The man whom she suspected of being Quentin smiled a queer smile at her. "But then, you're given to seeing werewolves, ghosts, and monsters, aren't you?"

"Why are you being so nasty to me?" she demanded.

"Am I?" he taunted her.

"Yes. Once you behaved like a friend. You were fond of Hazel. What has happened to change you? To make you act this way?"

"I haven't changed."

"You have," she accused him. "You're suddenly working hand in glove with Nicholas Freeze! What do you two have in common?"

"I'd mind my business if I were you," Mike snapped.

And then she said it, the thing she'd promised not to say. "Perhaps I know more than you guess," she warned him. "Maybe I know who and what you really are."

Mike came to her with three quick steps and seized her wrist in a cruel grip. "What did you say?"

At once she knew her mistake. "Nothing," she faltered.

"I heard you," he said in a taut voice. "Are you suggesting that I'm some sort of impostor?"

"I'll let you decide that," she retorted with a hint of defiance. But she was frightened now, and sorry she had so nearly revealed her feeling that he was Quentin.

His eyes burned into her angrily. "You cause trouble for me, and I promise you I'll cause plenty for you."

She made no reply, for at that moment Mr. Freeze had joined them again. He had come down the stairs during their argument, and now he peered at her with angry eyes.

"There's no one up there," he said icily.

"I saw Hazel."

"You saw nothing!" he said with disgust. "Go home. I oughtn't to have asked you to work tonight. You're just a silly girl with a case of nerves."

She didn't wait for a second invitation to leave. She was too anxious to get away from the sinister old barn. The memory of the ghostly features of Hazel and her painful moaning continued to haunt her as she got in the station wagon and drove to the City Hall auditorium.

The play was clearly over when she reached the auditorium. There were only a few cars in the parking lot and no one standing around on the sidewalk in front of the building. But the lights were all on, and so she felt the members of the company might still be changing, so she'd be able to contact Barnabas before he left.

The first person she met was the box office girl. And she asked her, "Has Mr. Barnabas Collins left the theatre?"

The blonde girl smiled. "Yes. About five minutes ago. He chatted with me for a minute on the way out."

Disappointment surged through her. "Did he happen to say where he was going?"

"No," the girl said. "We just talked about the play. I was telling him how much everyone likes him in it. Don't you think he's a wonderful actor?"

"Yes," she said, not half listening.

"That trace of a British accent," the girl went on with enthusiasm, "and he's so handsome, anyway. I hope he plays in more of our shows."

"Who else is here?" Carolyn asked.

The girl considered. "Most of the others."

"Jim Swift?"

"Yes. He hasn't left yet."

"I'll go on up and let him know I'm here," Carolyn said.

"You can ask backstage," the girl told her. "The stage manager will get him for you. Jim's nice-looking and a good actor, but I prefer Barnabas."

Carolyn continued on her way to the auditorium without waiting to give the girl any answer. She was too upset to be polite. The vision of Hazel's ghost was still frighteningly real in her mind. She'd wanted to get advice from Barnabas. Now she'd have to be content with what counsel she'd get from Jim. He was nice enough, but she didn't depend on him the way she did on her cousin.

Reaching the dark, empty auditorium, she was reminded of that other night when the werewolf figure had risen from between the aisles. Slightly fearful she hurried down the center aisle to the stage and the entrance to backstage at the right. Back there things were lively enough with the stage manager and his two assistants working at painting the scenery flats for the next week's play.

At her request one of the men went to the dressing room area to advise Jim Swift that she was waiting for him.

A few minutes later Jim appeared wearing light slacks and a brown sweater. "I've learned these Maine summer nights can be cool," he said with a smile as he joined her.

"I hope you don't mind my coming to pick you up," she said.

"I'm glad you've come," Jim said. "I've been thinking about you and how you've been making out since you lost Hazel."

Mention of her dead friend's name brought back the incident of the ghost. Carolyn shuddered. "Let's go where we can talk."

"The hotel coffee shop? It's usually deserted at this time of night."

"Fine," she agreed.

Five minutes later they sat at a table in a dimly lighted corner of the nearly empty coffee shop. Carolyn began her account of having seen the ghost of Hazel. Jim listened intently and when she finished, he said, "You seem very sure you saw a ghost!"

"I did."

"Though the others deny it."

"I expected them to," she said. "But I did see Hazel."

"What do you think her appearance meant?"

"I believe she was trying to warn me about some danger," Carolyn suggested.

"That could well be," he agreed.

"I haven't been happy about continuing working at the barn," she said. "After tonight it will be even more difficult for me."

"Perhaps you should think about giving up that job."

"Barnabas feels I should stay on and see what I can discover."

A brief shadow crossed Jim's pleasant face. "Barnabas again! You live by his rules, don't you?"

"That's not so," she protested, but not very convincingly. Barnabas did play a large part in her decisions. She added, "He managed to get away before I arrived tonight."

Jim smiled bitterly. "So that's why you suddenly turned to me? You missed Barnabas."

She crimsoned. "At least be happy you were second choice."

"My usual role," he said wryly. "Forgive me for wishing I could be the number-one man in your life."

"I've more important things to talk about than romance," she protested.

His eyes mocked her. "Are there more important things?"

"I'd say so. The truth about Hazel's death for one, and the reason why Mike Buchanan and Nicholas Freeze are suddenly so friendly."

Jim said, "I may have the answer to that."

"Tell me!"

"They probably think they can be of assistance to each other in amassing a fortune with that potion of youth. We're having a star appear in the next play. Marjorie Mason is arriving later in the week. Ever hear of her?"

"I've seen her in the late movie on television," Carolyn recalled. "She was an attractive redhead, but isn't she getting old?"

"She's over fifty, and not making movies these days. That's the reason she's doing straw-hat theatre." He paused significantly. "I'd say she'd be a prime prospect for that youth potion Freeze has. And who better to introduce her to Freeze than Mike Buchanan?"

"Who has to be Quentin Collins!"

"Probably," Jim Swift said. "From your accounts of him, he's an unfortunate who invariably winds up getting himself in trouble."

"Sometimes he deliberately causes the trouble," she said.

"I wouldn't know. But then you've met him."

She shook her head. "Not really. It's just that I've heard so much about him I feel I must know him. This story you tell about Marjorie Mason coming may be the answer to his being so thick with Freeze. You think they'll try to sell her on the youth potion?"

"She's ripe for it. An aging, beautiful actress desperate to lengthen her career."

"But they'd be taking a terrible chance," she worried. "Suppose the potion should kill her, as it did Hazel."

Jim shrugged. "No doubt your drunken Dr. Blake has convinced himself that that was due to an error in treatment They've likely planned a different series of injections."

She stared at him. "If she comes here, she should be warned."

"I'm not sure it would do any good. If she makes up her mind she wants the elixir, she's not liable to listen to our warnings."

"It frightens me to think of what may happen."

"There is one possibility," he said. "I understand that she's a friend of your cousin, Barnabas. Perhaps he could tactfully give her the background of the potion and let her know the desperate chance she'd be taking."

Carolyn brightened. "That's a good idea. I'll talk to Barnabas about it."

"There's one catch."

"What?"

"Barnabas is in trouble here in the village himself," Jim told her. "Another girl was attacked last night – one of the village girls.

That always gets the local people badly upset. Barnabas is being whispered about, and you can feel the hostility toward him on stage. The moment some of the audience recognize him, a murmuring starts."

Carolyn was concerned. "It's actually that bad?"

He nodded. "The curse of Collinwood is a main topic of conversation these days. The banning of the first Barnabas Collins from the estate has always been a legend here. And I heard Mike Buchanan making some taunting remarks to our Barnabas the other night."

"That sounds like Mike," she said.

"I was a little surprised," Jim admitted. "Mike made this snide remark to Barnabas about how he enjoyed sleeping through the daytime in a coffin."

She caught her breath. "What did Barnabas answer?"

"He took it very calmly," Jim said. "Told Mike he'd been paying too much attention to the Collinwood legends, and walked away. But there's bad feeling between those two, and I understand Barnabas has refused to do any more roles with the company."

"That's the company's loss," she said.

"I couldn't agree more."

"I hate to drive home alone after seeing that apparition," she worried. "It's one of the main reasons I came here looking for Barnabas."

Jim smiled across the table with her. "I'll go with you."

"But that would leave you stranded at Collinwood and not here at your boarding house."

"I'll manage. I can stay the night at Mike's cottage out there. I have before."

"Will he mind?"

"No, he has plenty of extra room."

She gave a small sigh of relief. "I would be glad to have the company."

"Then it's settled," he said.

The drive to Collinwood passed quickly with Jim beside her. When they reached the cottage, she halted the car to let him out. He gave her a tender look and leaned close to kiss her.

"Acting as understudy for Barnabas is better than not being near you at all," he told her wryly.

She smiled at him in the semi-darkness of the car. "You know I like you, too," she said.

"But Barnabas is really your romantic hero."

"Don't try to make up my mind for me," she protested.

Jim's face had a humorous yet sad expression. "I suppose it might be worse. You could have fallen in love with that other Collins renegade, Quentin."

"Mike Buchanan!" she exclaimed with disdain. "He's not my type at all! And the way he's behaved lately has made me especially dislike him."

"You're sure you'll be all right to drive the rest of the way?"

"Yes. It's only a short distance. You can see Collinwood from here."

Jim stared at the distant lights of the sprawling old mansion. "So you can," he agreed.

They said their final goodnights, and he left the car, while she drove on.

Nothing of event happened later that night or in the several days and nights that followed. Barnabas had suddenly decided to make himself unavailable to her, and she had a shrewd suspicion that after his chores in the theatre he moved on to one of the neighboring villages where he could find a suitable victim to prey on without adding more kindling to the flames of indignation that were already rampant in Collinsport.

Mike Buchanan came to the barn antique shop nearly every day. Dr. Blake often joined him and Nicholas. Carolyn was sure that Jim Swift had been right and the three were planning to try to sell the aging star, Marjorie Mason, on the potion of youth. Posters were already up in many of the store windows in the village and vicinity announcing her appearance in a new comedy.

Carolyn's own mood was far from comic. She'd not revealed the appearance of Hazel's ghost to anyone but Jim Swift. Indeed, as time passed, the vision she'd had was fading from her mind. She didn't question that she'd experienced it, but she was beginning to wonder whether it had been merely a spirit presence or actually Hazel's phantom she had seen.

Nicholas Freeze had made no further mention of the unsettling incident. He was actually more friendly with her than formerly. She felt he was working hard to win her good will and because of his miserable nature could only suspect that he was doing this with an evil motive, though she hadn't yet been able to determine just what. She was still frightened of going up to the gallery alone. Whenever something was needed from there, she tried to prevail on Tom Buzzell to get it for her. He usually obliged, though his own visions had become a favorite topic with him.

He had also seen Hazel's ghost, he confided in low tones to Carolyn as if terrified that anyone would hear him. "I've seen her, too," he began.

"Seen who?" she pretended to be naïve.

"You know who," he spoke more urgently. "Miss Hazel. Late at nights she comes back here. I saw her upstairs once, and then one dark night she was standing by the safe in the boss's office."

"Did you tell Nicholas Freeze?"

He looked embarrassed. "Can you imagine me telling him that? You know what he'd say. He'd complain I was getting the D.T.'s."

"You've seen Hazel's spirit twice, then?"

"You bet."

She eyed the emaciated man sharply. "Did she try to tell you anything?"

"Nope. But she sort of moaned, if you know what I mean."

"I know what you mean," she said soberly. "She made the same sound when I saw her."

It was near the end of the week when Carolyn had her first glimpse of the former Hollywood star, Marjorie Mason. Mike brought the actress to the antique barn late in the afternoon. The description Jim had given her of the aging beauty had been reasonably accurate. Marjorie Mason still had charm, but her beauty was fading.

Carolyn was standing by a Hudson Valley chest with four drawers and bun feet when the actress approached her with Mike. "That's an interesting chest," she exclaimed, bending down to inspect it. She asked Carolyn a few more questions about the 1880-vintage item, but it was Carolyn's impression that the actress was not really interested in antiques.

Her feelings in this regard were borne out later when Mike Buchanan led the star into Nicholas Freeze's office for a meeting with the antiques dealer and Dr. Blake. They were in there for a long time, but kept their voices low so that Carolyn had no chance to hear what they were saying.

But when Marjorie Mason emerged from the office on Mike's arm, it was obvious that she was in an excited state. And later when the director and the star had gone, Carolyn heard Nicholas and the drunken doctor laughing and joking together. Their mad greed sickened her. It was incredible that they'd so soon forgotten Hazel and what their experiment with the dangerous elixir had meant for her.

Carolyn still hoped that the star could be warned in time to save her. But when she heard her say, during an interview on the Ellsworth radio station, that she was going to remain in Collinsport to rest for a week or two after her appearance in the show, it became clear that Nicholas Freeze and the others had talked the fading beauty into trying the potion. Jim Swift's prediction had come true.

Carolyn was worried about Barnabas and anxious to talk to him, but he still kept away from the main house at Collinwood. She went over to the old house several evenings at dusk, but missed him every time. On Saturday night there was a bright full moon, and she decided to take a late evening walk along the cliffs. Normally she did not venture from the lawn area after dark, but this was such a magnificent night she decided to make it an exception.

She walked directly to the cliff and stood there for a few minutes admiring the pale moon riding high above the ocean. All the coastline was lighted in its glow, and she could see the rocks along the shore clearly. She began walking in the direction of Widows Hill. It was the high point along the cliffs and one of the interesting places on the estate.

Her thoughts were of the developments at the antique barn and whether Nicholas Freeze and Dr. Blake would be successful in their project of trying the elixir of life on Marjorie Mason. It seemed an incredibly long while ago she'd first stumbled on the secret compartment in the ancient desk and found the mysterious liquid and the warning that went with it.

John Wykcliffe must have been playing some macabre joke on future generations when he left the three bottles of the potion along with his various claims as to its powers. Already one person – Hazel – had lost her life because of it.

There was a gentle wind that brought a chilling breeze to her like the touch of a spectral hand. She was standing on the high point of land with the waves crashing against the rocks a hundred feet below. Under the moonlight the spot had beauty, but in a strange way it also had menace. It was here that the shipwrecks of Collinsport fisherfolk first became known. Here was where the waiting women gathered to watch for the returning boats, some of which were doomed never to return.

An eerie sense of fear shot through her. She had the feeling that eyes were fixed on her. Ghostly eyes! She couldn't imagine why this sensation of horror had come to her. But it had. Widows Hill was all at once a frightening place. The eyes seemed to be on her back, and so she turned very slowly to see who it might be.

Hazel was standing there! Hazel in the flowing white nightgown, her eyes staring, a slender hand upraised in a gesture of reaching out. At the sight of the ghost Carolyn called out her dead friend's name.

"Hazel!" she cried in near hysteria.

The phantom seemed to waver in the moonlight and then turned and fled across the field toward a clump of bushes. Carolyn hesitated, still stunned by the unexpected vision, and then she began to pursue the ghostly figure. By this time Hazel had vanished.

Carolyn raced on until she struck an uneven spot in the field and painfully turned her ankle in such a way as to send her stumbling forward.

She protected herself from the fall with her hands and then sat in the fairly deep grass for a few minutes as she massaged her aching ankle and considered whether or not to try to follow the ghost of Hazel. In the end she decided against it as a futile effort.

She was still sitting there when she heard footsteps approaching, and she looked up to see Barnabas come striding toward her, his caped coat outlined against the moonlit sky and his cane swinging in his hand.

Scrambling to her feet, she exclaimed, "Barnabas!"

He came to her. "What are you doing alone out here?"

"Walking and looking for you."

He smiled. "Then you've found me."

"Just a few minutes ago I saw someone else for the second time – someone you won't believe!"

"Who?"

"Hazel."

"Hazel!" He repeated, staring at her incredulously.

"I should say her ghost," Carolyn said, wincing a little as she tried to put some weight on her aching ankle. "I've been wanting to talk to you about it, but I haven't been able to locate you. There are other awful things in the making as well!"

CHAPTER 11

Barnabas looked concerned as he stood there in the moonlight with her. He said, "Is your ankle hurting badly? Do you feel up to walking as far as the bench on Widows Hill?"

She put her weight on the injured ankle and found it was not too painful. "I'll be all right," she said.

"Take my arm and lean on me for support," Barnabas advised. "It's better to favor the ankle, even if the harm is slight."

Gratefully she took his arm. They slowly made their way back to the high point of the cliffs and sat down on the bench. Only then did they make any attempt to resume their conversation.

She looked into his sympathetic face with troubled eyes. "It's been so long since we've had a chance to discuss things alone. Where have you been?"

"I have found it expedient to journey to some of the surrounding areas," he told her quietly.

"I thought it was probably something like that I've heard of the increasing whispers and suspicions concerning you here. The logical thing to do was make yourself scarce for a while."

He nodded. "As soon as I finished my week in the play, I told Mike Buchanan not to count on me for further parts. Then I began leaving Collinsport in the evenings."

She said, "Things are much worse here. I'm positive Mike and

Nicholas Freeze have persuaded that actress to have Dr. Blake treat her with the potion."

"You mean Marjorie Mason?"

"Yes. Isn't she a friend of yours? Jim said so."

"I worked with her in London years ago, but we are not close friends."

"Surely she'd listen to a warning from you!"

Barnabas looked sad. "I doubt it. Marjorie is very vain, and if Freeze and the others hold out a hope of returning her youth, she's very likely to go along with their scheme."

Carolyn was shocked to hear this from Barnabas. She'd hoped that he would have enough influence with the star to caution her against Mike and his associates. She said, "But surely it would make a difference if you let her know what happened to Hazel – that her own father killed her by giving her the potion!"

"We may believe that," Barnabas reminded her, "but the death certificate stated she died from natural causes."

"Dr. Blake falsified it, of course."

"No question," Barnabas said, "but we would find it hard to prove."

Carolyn stared out at the moonlit ocean. "Then we'll have to stand by and see them destroy Marjorie Mason!"

"Perhaps she won't be doomed as Hazel was," he suggested. "It may be that Dr. Blake is now aware of the dangers of John Wykcliffe's magic potion. He may use it with more discretion this time."

Carolyn turned to him again. "Do you think that's possible?"

"Yes."

"And if that isn't the case?"

"Then there will be another tragedy."

"How will they cover up for themselves if things go wrong again?" Carolyn demanded anxiously.

"I haven't any idea."

"Won't you at least try to warn Marjorie Mason of her danger?"

"I'll try," Barnabas said. "I'll go to the theatre and talk to her. But don't count on anything."

She sighed unhappily. "Of course, it's all that Quentin, or Mike Buchanan, or whatever you like to call him."

His deep-set eyes searched her face. "You're convinced that Quentin has taken over the master-minding of what is going on?"

"Yes. Jim Swift is watching him for me, but Quentin is wily."

"I won't dispute that," Barnabas said.

She stared at him in the semi-darkness. "Suppose the elixir works? That Marjorie Mason is rejuvenated? What then?"

"Then Nicholas Freeze and the others will reap a fortune.

From show business people alone they can get all the customers they can handle. Then there are the aged wealthy from every walk of life. What one of them wouldn't pay a king's ransom to regain their youth?"

"So they are playing for high stakes."

"The highest," he said.

"But there is only a limited amount of the potion. Just those three bottles. It can't possibly last long."

"Perhaps Dr. Blake is working on the formula for it. He may be able to analyze and duplicate its content. He's drunken and old, but he apparently had good training."

She nodded. "I believe that's true."

"If he isn't able to produce the potion, he will be all the more anxious to sell the scant supply to the highest bidders. And the bids could be fantastically high."

Carolyn shuddered. "I wouldn't touch it after what happened to Hazel. Tonight her phantom appeared in the field here. It was chasing her that gave me this injured ankle."

"You're positive you saw her ghost?"

"I am. Do you doubt it?"

"Perhaps. It's the kind of mistake any of us could make."

"I saw her," Carolyn said firmly. "I'm sure she's trying to give me a warning, to let me know the elixir caused her death."

"An unhappy, restless spirit," he said.

"I can hardly bear to remain at the barn working for that hateful old man," she complained, "knowing what he callously did to Hazel."

Barnabas said, "Still, you're in a better position to observe him by remaining there."

"He's a despicable character!"

"I agree," Barnabas said. "His god is money, and he's ready to sacrifice anyone or anything to it."

"He has no real love for the wonderful antiques he gathers for sale," she lamented. "To him they represent so much money, and that's all."

Barnabas smiled sadly. "If he had no sentiment where his daughter was concerned, you mustn't expect him to show it in his business."

"That's true," she agreed. "And with Dr. Blake and Quentin to aid and abet him, his evil knows no bounds."

Barnabas stared out at the silver ocean thoughtfully. "I'm puzzled that Mike, or Quentin, is playing such a major role in this. He is rather likable at most times. It is surprising that he mixed himself up in this roguery."

"Hasn't he done things like this before?"

"Rarely," Barnabas said. "The harm he has inflicted on previous occasions has been of a different variety."

She frowned. "I'm not sure I understand."

"I'm not making myself too clear," Barnabas admitted. "What about Jim Swift?"

"He's turned out to be the nicest person in the theatre company."

"You were very suspicious of him at first," Barnabas reminded her. "How could you have made such an error?"

She shrugged. "I decided he was Quentin without giving it proper thought or testing him to find out. Time has shown me my mistake."

"Now you're close friends?"

"I've turned to him whenever you're not around. He's the only other one I can count on," she said solemnly.

Barnabas looked at her very directly. "Have you fallen in love with him?"

"No."

"But you could if you let yourself?" he suggested.

She was confused. "I haven't considered that!" She wished that Barnabas hadn't brought the subject up.

"Is it because of me, you haven't thought of him in a romantic light?" He continued to question her relentlessly.

Carolyn blushed. "I don't know. Maybe."

"Then you are making a mistake," he told her quietly.

Her eyes were defiant. "Why should you say that? Don't you care for me at all?"

"I love you very much," Barnabas said.

"Well, then?"

"But there is no future for us. There might be one for you with him."

Feeling thoroughly unhappy, she demanded, "How can you talk like that?"

"You saw me in my casket," he reminded her. "Would you like to share that horror with me?"

"I wouldn't mind."

"You'd soon tire of the only life I could offer you," Barnabas warned her.

"But you may be cured of the curse of the vampire one day," she argued.

His eyes were sad. "I have been temporarily cured several times. My hopes rose high. But on each occasion I slipped back into my present state."

"I still feel something can be done for you."

"I hope you're right," Barnabas said. "But in the meantime I suggest you turn to Jim Swift. If he wants to marry you, and you like him well enough, you mustn't hold back because of anything you feel for me."

She got up from the bench. "Take me home. I don't want to hear any more."

Barnabas also rose. "You're angry with me. I'm only trying to do my best for you," he said gently as he briefly caressed her forehead with his cold lips.

"Kiss me on my lips, Barnabas," she demanded.

"You want to make it harder for both of us," he warned her. But he did as she asked, and though his lips were icy, the embrace filled her with a feeling of contentment and happiness nothing else could.

They walked back to Collinwood together, neither of them saying much. That night her sleep was restless and filled with dreams of the dead Hazel coming to her and trying to warn her of something. Waking, she saw the morning was bleak and foggy, which almost perfectly matched her depressed mood.

When she arrived at the antique barn, Nicholas Freeze was nowhere around, although it was early in the morning. She found Tom in the rear of the lower section laboriously polishing a Windsor chair. He paused in his labors to give her a nod of welcome.

"Where is Mr. Freeze?" she asked.

Tom gave her a knowing wink. "Gone over to Dr. Blake's."

"At this time of the day? It's only a few minutes after nine."

"I heard him talking on the phone," Tom said. "Him and Doc Blake. He said something about that actress going over to the Doc's place and that he'd meet 'em there."

Carolyn listened with growing alarm. So the treatments had likely begun for Marjorie Mason! Probably at this very minute Dr. Blake was injecting the insidious poison into the veins of the actress. She said, "They're up to something."

"Count on that," Tom said, folding the polishing rag in his hand. "Old Nick ain't one to waste time."

She sighed. "It's a wonder Mike Buchanan wasn't around."

"Not this morning," Tom said. "Though he's here often enough. I don't like that fella."

Carolyn offered him a rueful smile. "Neither do I."

Tom took a step closer to her and in a confidential voice said, "Something happened last night."

She stared at his gaunt face in the shadows. "What?"

"I saw her ghost again. Hazel's."

His news startled her, for she believed she had also seen her friend's ghost. She said, "Are you sure?"

"You betcha," the handyman said. "I was up in the gallery, and all of a sudden she came walking out of the shadows. Looked just like she did when she was alive, maybe a bit paler, and then she had on a nightgown."

His description exactly matched that of the Hazel she'd seen drifting across the lawn toward her. She said, "Did she try to talk to you?"

"Made a moaning sound," Tom said, "and then she moved behind a lot of piled-up stuff, and when I tried to follow her, there wasn't a sign of her. I was so upset I ran downstairs and told old Nick."

"What was his reaction?"

"About what I expected. He got mad and started shouting I was crazy from drinking!"

"A predictable way for him to show his anger."

"I said it had nothing to do with drinking. Then he went upstairs himself. He stayed up there a few minutes and came down in a kind of state. Do you know what I think?"

"Tell me," she urged.

He held up a skinny forefinger. "I think he saw her ghost, too."

It was a new idea, but not too preposterous. "Why do you say that?"

"Because he was real shook up and went out right away. He was still gone when I closed up the place. I say he was shocked."

"You could be right," she admitted. "And I do believe Hazel's ghost is restless and around. I saw her on the lawn at Collinwood late last night."

"There you are!" Tom exclaimed, delighted at having his phantom visions confirmed.

"What's all this nonsense about ghosts?" Nicholas Freeze suddenly appeared behind them, so suddenly that they both turned to gaze at him in consternation.

Tom Buzzell found his voice first. He quavered, "We weren't meaning any harm, boss. We were just comparing notes."

"I'll not have time I pay for wasted in such nonsensical conversation," he said sarcastically.

"We were only chatting for a moment," Carolyn said.

"I expect better from you than from that crazy character," he said, his wrinkled face showing his anger.

"I'm sorry," she said.

"You should be," he replied. Turning to Tom, he ordered, "You finish with those chairs. They're due to be delivered by noon."

"Yes, sir," Tom said, kneeling to resume his industrious polishing.

"You come along with me. I've got in a new shipment that has to be catalogued," he told Carolyn.

She followed him to the doorway of the barn, where a load of furniture and oddments had just been delivered. Under his direction she listed a 'Governor Hepplewhite drop-leaf table, an Early American armchair, several small tables, a collection of Canton china, and some Currier & Ives prints. She went into the office with him after they'd finished.

He waved her to a chair. "I'm sorry I lost my temper when I found you talking to Tom," he said.

"It's all right," she said quietly.

He stood uneasily by his desk. "I'd prefer to be friends with you. In many ways you remind me of Hazel. Having you here is good for me."

"I'm willing to stay on for the rest of the summer," she said.

"Excellent!" Mr. Freeze said. "I still feel the loss of my daughter most grievously. I hope you believe that."

She was by no means sure, but she wished to preserve the improved relations between them, so she said politely, "I'm positive you must."

He frowned and took a few steps across the office, then paused and turned to say, "It pains me when that fool Tom goes around insisting he sees her ghost."

"Perhaps he thinks he does," Carolyn said tactfully.

"His mind is addled enough with alcohol for him to believe anything," Nicholas said with disgust. "But if he keeps on with this I'll have to discharge him."

"I'm sure he means no harm."

"But he does harm! He got your nerves going so you thought you saw her up there the other night. I won't have it!" Mr. Freeze insisted.

Fortunately, at that point a customer came to look at chinaware and brass, and she was able to escape his angry ramblings. There had been a frightened something in his manner which she didn't fully understand and which she intended to discuss with Barnabas. That couldn't be until evening, and meanwhile she had a busy day to face at the barn. On these dull, foggy days the tourists filled their time by visiting the antiques shops and art galleries. Usually they bought at least some small item.

She left the barn briefly at lunchtime to walk to the hotel coffee shop. She decided to save time by sitting at the counter for quick service. She'd no sooner sat down and ordered than Mike Buchanan came to occupy the stool next to her.

He gave her a cold smile. "We seem to be always meeting each other at unexpected times."

"Yes," she said, primly.

Mike continued to eye her. "You're in a subdued mood today, and you never come to the theatre lately."

She said, "Barnabas isn't acting there any more."

"Is he your only interest? What about Jim Swift? He has a good part this week."

"I've not had time to go to the theatre," she said.

"Don't tell me old Nicholas is making you work every night?" he taunted her.

She stared at her plate, wishing she could escape him, or that he'd leave her alone. She said, "I have other things to do at home."

"I suppose you do," he said. "I don't have as much chance to meet you at Collinwood since Roger forbade me to venture near the house on my midnight strolls."

She took a sip of her coffee, then left her money for the lunch and slid from her stool. "I have to get back to work," she said.

"Hope I didn't make you rush away?" he said with one of his tormenting smiles.

"You didn't," she replied, but in fact he had. She walked quickly out of the coffee shop and headed back to the barn. Any doubts she had left that Mike Buchanan was Quentin Collins had long since vanished.

She found it hard to understand why Barnabas didn't more wholeheartedly agree with her. Whenever she mentioned this to him, he kept pointing out that Quentin was a misunderstood rather than a truly evil character. He was dangerous only when under the spell of the werewolf curse. Her experience with Mike didn't bear this out. It seemed Mike had a broad streak of evil. She felt that Barnabas was being too kind to the renegade Collins cousin.

It was an exhausting day, and the fog was still thick as she drove home. At Collinwood there was an air of restlessness. She found Roger and her mother in the rear parlor in serious conversation when she joined them. The two looked up at her, and there was a moment of embarrassed silence.

She was forced to ask, "Am I interrupting something?"

Roger stood up. "Nothing you shouldn't hear. It's about time you took it on yourself to share some of the family burdens."

Her mother stared up at them plaintively. "I don't think you need worry Carolyn with this!"

Roger frowned at her. "I disagree."

He turned to Carolyn, saying, "Of course you've heard us talk about Quentin and the problems he has raised here at Collinwood from time to time."

"Yes," she said in a small voice.

"It seems we aren't to be rid of him yet," Roger went on with annoyance. "I had a call from the police again today. This time it wasn't Barnabas they wanted to question me about – he seems to have been behaving himself for a little at least – but about Quentin."

She stared at her uncle's angry face. "Do you really think Quentin is here?"

"Not at Collinwood," Roger replied, "but in the village."

"That is just a surmise on your part," Elizabeth rebuked him.

Carolyn had it on the tip of her tongue to add that she knew more about the Quentin problem than he did. She and Barnabas had figured it all out – Quentin was living at Collinwood under the name of Mike Buchanan. She knew to go on with this would only infuriate her uncle more, so she said nothing.

"The police have assured me that Quentin is around," Roger said. "Several people have seen him in his werewolf transformation during these past few moonlit nights."

"People imagine things. The police aren't always right," her mother objected.

"I say they are, this time," was Roger's reply.

"What can we do about it?" Carolyn asked her uncle.

"Very little beyond keeping a watch for him," Roger admitted.

"That is why I say it's pointless to drag Carolyn into this," Elizabeth said unhappily.

Roger looked stern. "I disagree. I felt it my duty to warn her."

"Thank you, Uncle Roger," she said. "Have you any suspicion of who Quentin is pretending to be?"

"Not really," he admitted. "I imagine he's here in the guise of a tourist. He's bound to keep well out of my way. I'd be able to spot him in a moment."

"But Barnabas claims he's an expert at disguise," she said.

"He is," her mother agreed. "He's returned here many times and never been recognized."

"Because we weren't on the alert," Roger maintained. "Now we know he's here, and we can watch for him."

"What did the police have to say?" Carolyn asked. "Has he done anyone harm?"

"He's frightened several old ladies and a girl half to death," Roger snapped. "Seeing him with his face distorted in one of his seizures isn't very pleasant. I hope you're never exposed to it."

Again Carolyn had to hold her silence, for she had been exposed to that monster face twice – in the theatre auditorium and later at Collinwood. She drew some small comfort from the word that the police were watching for Quentin. It meant that sooner or later Mike Buchanan would be suspected and they might close in on him before the injections to the actress were completed.

She said, "I hope the police catch him."

"Or at least frighten him away," Elizabeth said. "I hate to

think of Quentin in trouble again. In many ways I'm fond of him."

"Mistaken sentiment!" Roger snapped.

That was the end of the talk, but as soon as dinner was over, Carolyn slipped out of the house. Wearing a light raincoat draped over her shoulders, she crossed the fog-shrouded lawns and made her way to the old house. She wanted to get there before Barnabas left, if possible. The coming of night, together with the thick mist, had made everything seem menacing. The limbs of the tall shade trees showed eerily through the fog, stretched toward the sky like ghostly black hands clutching at some unseen presence. Visibility was reduced to a distance of only a few feet, so that any view of the outbuildings was shut off from her.

As she neared the shuttered red-brick old house in which Barnabas lived with his servant, Hare, it seemed to rise from a sea of fog. Everything else around it was blotted out. She mounted the wet steps and used the brass knocker to announce her arrival. Soon heavy steps sounded in the corridor and the stout, unshaven Hare showed his coarse face in the doorway. She told him she wanted to see Barnabas, and with some reluctance he let her in.

She followed him down the dark hallway, and he ushered her into the elegantly furnished living room. Barnabas often preferred candlelight, and on this occasion the room was lighted by two candles at either end of the mantelpiece and a candelabrum on the center of the table in the middle of the ornate room.

Hare gave her a sullen look and then vanished amid the shadows of the hallway. She moved to the fireplace and stood there in silent thought for a moment. Apparently she'd arrived before the departure of Barnabas, and she was glad of this. Lately he'd been leaving Collinwood early in the evening to forage for the blood necessary for his survival in one of the surrounding villages. By moving about in this way he'd eased the talk in Collinsport and been able to get by.

She wanted to tell him what Roger had said, and also about her talks with Nicholas Freeze and Mike Buchanan.

She was thinking about all this when she heard his familiar step from the corridor and looked up to see him enter the room.

"You are here early," he said, somewhat tensely. And she noticed how weary he looked. He looked more gaunt than ever before.

"I had to see you," she said.

"I was on the point of leaving," Barnabas told her, and she saw that his eyes had a strange, almost fanatical, light in them.

"Aren't you well?" she asked. "You look so strange!"

Those weird eyes burned into her. "I wish you hadn't decided to come here," he said in a rather thick voice unlike his own.

"But there are things I've found out," she insisted. "Things I had to tell you about. The police are looking for Quentin, for one thing."

"Are they?" He seemed to be hardly listening to her, and she saw that his hands were working nervously.

"So Roger says. And they haven't found out that he's posing as Mike Buchanan, at least not according to Roger."

"Was I mentioned?"

"No," she said, "they seem to have lost their interest in you."

"Good," Barnabas said with a deep sigh. Then he came close to her and took her in his arms. "Close your eyes," he ordered her.

She stared into his tense face and knew that this was not the Barnabas she was so familiar with. "What has changed you?" she asked.

"Just close your eyes," he asked her.

She did so, and immediately she felt his cold lips on her neck. But this was no ordinary kiss! The icy touch of his lips took on a scalding sensation, and the intense burning made her feel weak and dizzy. Her head was spinning, and she lost all sense of awareness. Gradually she descended into an ocean of blackness.

It was a strange, soothing relaxation that overcame her. She floated in this lost place, remote from everything. The scalding at her throat had turned to an icy chill once more. She was drifting aimlessly in the night!

When she opened her eyes, she was in another of the shadowed rooms of the old house, stretched out on a divan. She saw Barnabas standing by her and raised herself up to say, "I'm sorry I made such a fool of myself by fainting."

The mad light had vanished from his eyes and now, in an easy voice, he told her, "You have no reason to apologize."

CHAPTER 12

Even though she was still slightly dazed, Carolyn was sure she knew what he meant. Her eyes met his. "So it was my throat this time," she said in a whisper.

"I never intended it that way," Barnabas said in a tragic tone.

Sympathy for him welled up in her. "You know that it makes no difference to me. I offered to help you."

"If you hadn't arrived when you did, it would have been all right," he told her wearily.

She reached out to take his hand in hers. "I'm happy about it Honestly! It makes me feel as if I've been able to do something for you."

"You have."

"Then let's forget about it," she said, for the first time aware of the stinging at her throat where Barnabas had taken the blood from her.

"I wish I could," Barnabas said, seating himself on the couch beside her.

"I have so much to tell you," she went on quickly, anxious to get away from the unpleasant topic. "Dr. Blake is already giving Marjorie Mason the elixir-of-life injections."

"I know."

"Have you talked with her?"

"Yes. My hunch was right. She wouldn't listen to me. She's too greedy to regain her youth."

"Does she know the risk she's taking?"

"She thinks there isn't any, and I wasn't able to convince her to the contrary."

Carolyn gave him a despairing look. "So we'll have to wait and see what comes out of it."

"That's all we can do," Barnabas agreed.

"I'm frightened," she said.

"Don't be," Barnabas told her. "It won't do any good. We can only hope that Dr. Blake will use some judgment this time."

"That drunken man isn't responsible," she said with scorn.

"Let me see you back to Collinwood," Barnabas said. "I don't want you walking alone in this fog."

"But we haven't had any real chance to talk," she protested.

He was on his feet "I'm afraid it's all the time I can spare, for now. I want to go to the village and check on a few things."

She stood up and realized she was still feeling weak. "Can I help in any way?"

Barnabas gave her a fond smile. "You've done enough for one night. Just be careful not to let Roger see that red mark on your neck. You know how he feels about me."

She drew the raincoat about her in preparation for going out into the damp night. "Don't worry! He'll never find out."

Barnabas was in a subdued mood as he escorted her back to Collinwood. He refused to go inside and kissed her goodnight at the door. She watched him vanish in the heavy gray mist before she went into the house.

Elizabeth was coming down the stairway as she entered. "My!" she said. "You look white! Did you have some kind of scare?"

"No," she said, careful to keep her hand up to her throat to cover that tell-tale scar.

"Are you ill?" her mother asked, coming down to her.

"No, I'm fine," she replied nervously.

"Well, you don't look it," was her mother's comment.

"I think I'm overtired," she said. "I'm going to bed early."

"That could be wise," Elizabeth agreed "By the way there was a phone call for you when you were out."

"Oh? Who was it?"

"One of the actors at the theatre," her mother said. "I believe he told me his name was Jim."

"Jim Swift!"

"That's it," she agreed. "He seemed anxious to talk to you, and when I said you'd gone out for a little, he told me he'd call when the play was over. I imagine that will be around eleven."

"I'll wait up for the call," Carolyn said.

Elizabeth studied her with troubled eyes. "You look as if you needed a rest. I wouldn't stay up just to take the call. I can ask the young man to phone you in the morning."

"No, I'd rather wait for it," Carolyn insisted.

And so she did. Long after both Roger and her mother had gone upstairs she remained in the living room waiting to get Jim Swift's call. It came promptly after eleven.

"Is that you, Carolyn?" he asked.

"Yes."

"When I called before, you were out."

"Yes. Mother gave me your message."

"I didn't know where to try to reach you," he said.

"I've been waiting."

The voice at the other end of the line sounded worried. "There's been a development I thought you should know about. Marjorie Mason is very ill at her boarding place."

"Where is she staying?"

"She's moved to Dr. Blake's."

Her comment was grim. "Lovely!"

"I think it's the same story." His voice was troubled. "The elixir isn't agreeing with her."

"How will they cover up if she dies?"

"I can't imagine," Jim said.

"Let me know if she gets worse," Carolyn said.

"If I know about it myself," Jim said. "I only found out this much by accident. One of the girls in the company went to visit Marjorie and found her ill."

"I see," she said.

"Where were you tonight?" he asked. "With Barnabas?"

She hesitated, then said, "Yes. For a short time."

"You know that makes me jealous," Jim said.

"Nonsense," she replied.

"It's true," the young actor said. "I want to see you soon. I have a lot to tell you."

"Anything about Mike Buchanan?"

"Nothing except what we both know. He's in on this deal to give the potion to Marjorie."

"I believe the police are watching him," she said.

"What makes you think so?" He sounded slightly surprised.

"They're looking for Quentin, though I'm not certain they have discovered that he is Quentin."

"It probably won't take long," Jim said. "Have you talked to them?"

"No."

"Better keep out of it."

"Do you honestly believe so?"

"I do. I'll have to go now," Jim said. "I may drop by the barn to see you."

"We can't talk there unless Nicholas Freeze is out," she warned him. "He's always eavesdropping."

"I'll remember that," he said. "And don't you forget I'm in love with you." With that tender sentiment expressed, he hung up.

The sun was bright again the following morning, and it was warm. Carolyn dressed and hurried down for breakfast to discover her mother and Roger at the table. The moment she sat down with them she was aware of an air of tension in the room.

Giving them an inquiring look, she asked, "Is something wrong?"

Her mother nodded. "Yes. Something tragic happened last night."

"What was it?" she demanded, at once afraid it might concern Barnabas. "Did Barnabas get in some trouble?"

"No," her Uncle Roger said with some disgust. "It has nothing to do with him or anyone we know."

"Well, then?"

"That actress, Marjorie Mason, drove her car over the cliffs last night," he explained. "They think she was trying to make a curve and the car went out of control."

Elizabeth went on to explain, "She'd been staying at Dr. Blake's since her appearance here. According to the word, she'd been ill. Dr. Blake says she must have had a high temperature when she left the house. In her confused state of mind she wasn't fit to drive."

Roger looked derisive. "Probably Blake was dead drunk, or she wouldn't have managed to get by him and go to her car. I'd call it a case of medical neglect."

"No one will ever come out and say it," Elizabeth predicted.

"Whether they do or not, I still say that's the story," Roger countered.

Carolyn listened to it all in a kind of daze. So that was how they'd solved the problem of the star falling victim to the elixir! They'd placed her body in her car and sent it careening over the cliffs to make it seem an accident. Another murder accounted for. It made her ill just to think about it.

She said, "Do you think the authorities will investigate the accident?"

"They won't put themselves out," was Roger's opinion. "It's a clear enough case. No mystery there!"

She wanted to shout out that there was, but knew it would

be useless. So instead, she said meekly, "I suppose not."

When she went to work at the "Olde Antique Barn," she expected to find Nicholas Freeze in a dejected mood, since his second attempt to use the magic potion had failed. Her expectations proved to be right. As she entered the cool darkness of the barn, she heard him railing at Tom somewhere in the rear. Whenever the owner was in a rage, he worked it out on the unfortunate Tom.

Carolyn was at the desk in the office when the old man came in. She looked up and said, "Good morning."

"I wouldn't call it that, with that fool Tom putting the wrong finish on a fine mahogany table," Nicholas snorted.

"The sun is shining," she said. "And the fog has rolled out."

"We do better business with the fog," he said, sinking dejectedly into a plain chair.

Carolyn was watching him closely. She now spoke with deliberate malice to get his reaction, saying, "Wasn't that a tragic car accident last night?"

A funny look crossed his aged face. "What accident?"

"You must have heard about it," she insisted. "Marjorie Mason drove her car over a cliff. She was killed."

"News to me," he maintained, but she could tell by his expression he wasn't being truthful.

"She was staying at your friend's, Dr. Blake's," she told him.

Nicholas Freeze frowned. "Must call Blake and find out about it from him," he said carefully.

"Yes, you should," she agreed. The guilt on his face proved he knew the details all too well.

Later in the morning Mike Buchanan and the doctor arrived. Mike seemed his usual calm self, but the alcoholic Dr. Blake looked nothing less than shaken. He barely noticed Carolyn, though he was usually friendly to her.

Since there was no chance to overhear them, anyhow, she went to a distant part of the barn where Tom was dolefully at work restoring the finish of a mahogany circular table.

Going up to him, she said, "Did you hear about the accident, Tom?"

"Yes, Miss," the handyman said. "I heard old Nick raving about it on the phone to someone when I first came in this morning."

She raised her eyebrows. "He told me he hadn't heard about it until I told him."

"He was lying, same as usual. You ought to know him by now."

"I should."

"I reckon that daughter of his haunts this place to try and make him mend his ways, but it won't make any difference."

She stared at him. "Have you seen Hazel's ghost again?"

He nodded. "I had a bottle with me here last night. I worked late, then I sat in a dark corner and had me a few snorts, went to sleep for a mite. And would you believe it, when I woke up, she was there standing looking down at me. Her eyes were staring, and I thought she was going to say something. Instead of that, she turns and hurries away. I didn't see her again."

"That's a hard story to believe," she told him, though she knew she had seen the same phantom herself.

"Hazel is here," he insisted. "Her ghost has never left this place. Only trouble is the old man never seems to see it. And he's the one who should."

"Maybe he will, later," she suggested.

She left the workman and went out by the barn door again. She was talking to a customer when the doctor and Mike came out of the office with Mr. Freeze. Mike gave her a very definite nod before he left with the doctor. She wondered what conclusion they had come to at their council of war.

The day ended, and she returned to Collinwood. That evening Barnabas came to the house early. She sat with him in the garden while they discussed the star's tragic death.

Barnabas said, "Of course they poisoned her with the elixir just as they killed Hazel."

"We were almost sure it would happen."

"What will be their next move?" Barnabas wondered.

"Surely they'll give it up now," she reasoned. "They know it's a failure. I think John Wykcliffe knew that when he left the warning note with the three containers of the potion."

"Nicholas has built too much on the elixir to give up easily," said Barnabas.

"You think they'll try again?"

"Yes," he said. "Nicholas will convince himself that it is bungling on Dr. Blake's part that is responsible for their series of failures with the potion."

"I don't believe that's so. I'd say the potion is poisonous."

"Very likely," Barnabas agreed. "Perhaps a grim joke of John Wykcliffe's."

"I could go to the police and tell them," she suggested.

"They'd think you'd lost your mind. The story is too fantastic," he warned her.

"What can we do?"

"Wait and see which way they move this time."

"We did that before," she reminded him, "and Marjorie

Mason died."

"This time it will be different," he promised.

He remained with her until about ten o'clock, and then he left. She had an idea he would go on to one of the other villages in search of blood. She wished that he had taken it from her as he had on that other night. But she knew he had only succumbed to that temptation because his thirst had been overpowering.

The news of the day had been so upsetting she couldn't sleep. It was a fine warm night, and she returned to the garden for a stroll just before midnight. She'd only been there a few minutes when she saw a familiar figure walking toward her. It was Jim Swift!

She ran to meet him. "Jim! You're the last person I expected to see."

"I came back to the cottage with Mike," he told her, and he took her in his arms for a brief kiss. "That makes me feel better," he said with a smile.

"It's good to have you here," she told him.

His eyes held a twinkle. "I was afraid I might find you and Barnabas together."

"He left here fairly early," she said.

"That's the way I like it. What did he think about Marjorie Mason's death?"

"Probably the same as you. Both Barnabas and I feel sure the accident was staged. I'm sure she died from the poison and they faked the accident."

Jim nodded. "I think Mike arranged that part of it."

She looked at him imploringly. "They must be stopped somehow."

"I have an idea they'll overstep the bounds of safety soon," he said, with a confidence she couldn't understand. "The possession of an elixir of life has always sent its owners mad. Nicholas and his crowd are going to be no exceptions. They're due to commit some new crime that will trap them."

"I hope so," she said.

Jim looked puzzled. "There are things I don't understand. I told you a girl from the company went to visit Marjorie regularly and reported on her illness to the rest of us. She claims that the last time she saw Marjorie the poor woman was insane. She lay tossing in bed like a regular maniac."

"Hazel was like that," she said with some awe. "Then she seemed to go into a kind of trance. It must have been the poison."

"I wonder," Jim Swift said.

"I'd like to do something about it all, but Barnabas says I must have patience."

"For once I agree with Barnabas," Jim said. "But don't expect it to happen often."

She smiled ruefully. "I'm sure you like him."

"He has his qualities," Jim said. "He's a good actor, for one thing. But I don't see him as anyone you should consider romantically."

"Isn't that something I have to decide for myself?"

"Unfortunately, yes," he admitted. "I'll have to be on my way, or Mike will be asking me a lot of questions."

"What was your excuse for getting away from him?"

"I told him I wanted to enjoy the night air and the sound of the ocean."

"That sounds reasonable," she said.

"You don't know how Mike has changed," he said. "Suddenly he is very suspicious of everyone."

"Why don't we call him Quentin and have it done with?" she said impatiently. "We all know who he is!"

Jim smiled. "Remember the advice Barnabas gave you. Patience is the word."

After kissing her again he left. She went inside more confused than she had been before. Jim's charm was growing on her, yet she couldn't see herself deserting Barnabas to marry the young actor. She would prefer to wait; perhaps one day Barnabas would be cured and able to ask her to be his wife. He worried that a cure might not be permanent, but she was willing to take that chance. So Jim, however likable, could not be encouraged.

The summer days went by quickly. Darkness was coming sooner with the advent of August. Things settled down to a quiet, fairly normal routine. The tragic accident of Marjorie Mason was forgotten as new events came along to catch attention.

It was on a Friday night in late August when Mr. Freeze asked her to work late again. Since it was near the end of the season, and Tom was off on one of his drunks, she hesitated to refuse the request.

She waited on customers until the barn was closed at ten. Then she helped look after the closing details, checking the rear doors and windows of the barn to be sure they were locked. When this was done, she went to the dingy office where Nicholas Freeze was hunched over his desk.

"I've closed all the windows and doors and locked them," she said.

He got up. "Good girl."

"I'll go now, if there's nothing else," she said, offering this as a cue for him to pay her.

Instead he remained standing, staring at her with a weird gleam in his ancient eyes. In his reedy voice he said, "There is something else."

For no reason she understood, his words sent a stab of fear through her. "I don't understand."

He took a step toward her. He smiled evilly, revealing yellowed stubs of teeth. "Yes, you do. I know how you've been pretending innocence. You've made on you forgot about the elixir and the promise it offered. You've ignored the fact that because Blake gave my girl a wrong dose of it and she became ill."

Carolyn gasped. "You admit that?"

He nodded. "I don't mind telling you now. The same thing happened with Marjorie Mason. Blake wasn't quite sure of how much to give her, so we had to make it seem she perished in an auto accident."

"Why do you tell me all this?" she demanded.

"I'm being honest with you," Freeze said, "because we need your help. I want you to offer yourself for the third experiment. It can bring you eternal youth, and we'll share the profits with you."

"You're mad!" she faltered. "You want to kill me like the others!"

He shook his head sadly. "You're all wrong. The others didn't die from the potion. It sent them insane. Hazel isn't dead. I had Drape put rocks in her coffin. That's what you'll find buried in the cemetery! A coffin full of rocks!"

She gazed at him in terror. "Then the ghost Tom and I saw wasn't a ghost!"

"No. It was Hazel. I have her shut up in the house, but every so often she's gotten out on me, and that's the ghost you've been seeing! You and Tom!" He gave a harsh cackle of laughter.

Carolyn was horrified. "Don't you care?"

"Too late now," he quavered. "I need to prove the elixir a success. I'll see she gets the best care. Now it's up to you. Blake has developed a means to offer the full treatment with only one injection. We need someone healthy and young. Someone like you!"

"No!" she cried.

As she made this refusal, the office door opened and Dr. Blake and Mike Buchanan quietly walked in. They were filled with silent threat. She looked from Nicholas to them with mounting terror.

Mike stood by the door, his dark glasses covering his malevolent eyes, and instructed the doctor, "Go ahead, Blake. Let's get it over with quickly."

The drunken medico gave her an apprehensive glance as he

put down his bag on a nearby table and began opening it. "You'll not feel anything at all," he told her nervously. "I'm sure it will work this time!"

She backed away from the three, moving close to a wall of the shadowed, menacing office. "No," she begged in a frantic whisper. "No!"

"If it works we'll all be rich beyond belief. If it fails you'll only be mad – no worse off than Hazel!" Nicholas chuckled insanely.

"Please!" she begged Mike Buchanan now. "Don't let them!"

His smile was cold. "I'm in this too far," he said. He nodded to Dr. Blake, who was waiting with a hypodermic in his hand. "Go ahead!"

"No!" she screamed and ran to the door.

Mike was quick to intercept her and carry her back struggling toward the doctor. "Let's not have any more nonsense!" he snarled.

Carolyn saw the doctor's hand raised with the hypodermic in it She closed her eyes, unable to fight for her freedom any longer. In a moment the hypodermic needle would shoot the elixir of madness into her veins, and she'd be doomed like the others!

A shot rang out, and she opened her eyes to see Dr. Blake staggering back with a confused expression on his florid face. She also was barely conscious of the blood spurting through the cloth of his right sleeve. The hypodermic needle had fallen to the floor.

Mike let her go and wheeled on the intruder. Jim Swift stood in the doorway. He had fired the shot that had saved her.

"All right, Mike," Jim said calmly. "I'm going to be more generous with you than I should be. I'm counting to ten, and by then I want you out of here and on your way out of town. Ready?"

Mike glared at him and then at her. "You can't bluff me!" he said angrily.

"Don't go, Mike," Nicholas quavered.

"You can stay and explain to the police if you'd rather," Jim said, the gun still aimed at the director. "I'm starting to count."

Mike hesitated and then gave Nicholas a disgusted look. "What's the use?" he demanded. "We're finished!"

From the chair into which he'd slumped, Dr. Blake groaned, "Get help!"

Mike instead went to the door and ran out. Then Jim moved across to Nicholas Freeze and told him, "I should put a bullet in you as well. But I won't. Instead I'll let you answer charges for attempting to harm this girl and allow you to live and care for the daughter you've driven mad. But first there is one other task to finish." He went to the bag on the floor and took out the ancient bottles with the potion in them and used the butt of his gun to smash them all and send their contents spilling out on the floor. Then he crushed the hypodermic with his heel.

Nicholas Freeze collapsed into the chair behind his desk. Head in his hands, he began sobbing brokenly.

Jim moved to her. "As you see, the promise of eternal youth can be a vicious thing. It always brings men to madness, as it did with these three."

"Jim!" she moved to cling to him, ready to faint.

"Let me get you out of here," he said.

Carolyn remembered the details of what happened after that only vaguely. He put her in the station wagon before calling the police. Then he drove her home to an indignant and terrified Roger and Elizabeth.

She was safely in her room and in her own bed before he left. He came to her and said, "Feeling better now?"

"Much," she said. "What about Hazel?"

"They found her in the house," he said. "Hopefully with treatment she'll come back to herself. The doctor who examined her thinks her condition is only temporary."

"I'm so glad," she murmured and looked up at him fondly. "It was wonderful the way you got rid of Quentin."

He smiled. "I thought I did rather well. Quite a melodramatic scene. It appealed to my sense of good theatre."

"When will I see you again?"

"I'll be in touch soon," he promised, bending down to kiss her goodnight. Then with a look of tender amusement he lingered to add, "I think, for just once, I stole some of the thunder from Barnabas."

Carolyn was too weary to do anything but offer a weak smile. Then he left and she closed her eyes and slept. She expected to see him the following day, but when she phoned his boarding place in town she learned that he had left Collinsport. It was beyond her understanding.

Not until she met Barnabas in the garden at twilight did she discover why he had chosen to leave at his moment of triumph. Barnabas smiled at her sadly and said, "Now I'll tell you something I couldn't before."

"What?"

"Mike Buchanan wasn't Quentin. You were rescued by Quentin."

It came as a shattering surprise. "Jim Swift?"

"I knew almost from the beginning Quentin was posing as

Jim," Barnabas said.

"Because we're friendly rivals, I couldn't tell you."

She stared up into his sad, handsome face. "Now I understand so many things he told me. And he was always afraid I'd marry you. He claimed to be in love with me."

"I think he is," Barnabas said. "But like myself, he's not able to ask you to be his wife. At least, not yet."

"Will you ever be free?"

"Even a curse must have a life span," Barnabas said. "Let us hope that soon one of us can finally pledge his heart to you."

COMING SOON FROM
HERMES PRESS

Book Twenty-Six: *Barnabas, Quentin and the Body Snatchers*
Book Twenty-Seven: *Barnabas, Quentin and Dr. Jekyll's Son*
Book Twenty-Eight: *Barnabas, Quentin and the Grave Robbers*
Book Twenty-Nine: *Barnabas, Quentin and the Sea Ghost*
Book Thirty: *Barnabas, Quentin and the Mad Magician*
Book Thirty-One: *Barnabas, Quentin and the Hidden Tomb*
Book Thirty-Two: *Barnabas, Quentin and the Vampire Beauty*

DARK SHADOWS

Published by **Hermes** Press

AVAILABLE NOW
Dark Shadows: The Complete Series: Volume 1
SECOND EDITION
From the Gold Key Comics 1968-1970
www.hermespress.com

𝔇ARK 𝔖HADOWS

Published by **Hermes** Press

Visit **www.hermespress.com** to learn more
and see additional *Dark Shadows* titles.